WITH ONE LAST KISS

A Tragic Love Story

VIOLET HAZE

Stoked Publishing House

Front Cover Design by BookCoverZone
Back & Spine by Violet Haze
Stoked Publishing House
ISBN-13: 978-0-9992261-8-6
1st Edition: June 2019

PROLOGUE

THE END OF MY LIFE WASN'T FAR AWAY.

It was the truth. I laid on the floor staring up at the ceiling, which appeared to rotate in a clockwise manner, waiting to die.

My eyes struggled to remain open due to their heaviness. Not because I didn't want to close them, but because when I did, my life would be well and over.

The sleeping pills mixed with the liquor invaded my body. When the concoction finally worked as it should, well, my life would be no more.

And nobody would be coming to save me.

Honestly, there wasn't anybody close enough to me to gather I needed actual saving. Even if they understood the pain stabbing at my heart, I never showed it. Hiding behind a weak smile and an "I'm fine" attitude seemed to make others exhale with relief. Fine with me, since it kept them from saying ridiculous and unhelpful platitudes.

As if that mattered.

No amount of love would save me, because love is what would kill me. Literally. Being in love was an affliction, and there was nothing worse than having it to the degree I did.

The love of my life and I had the kind of love story that divided people. They sighed with envy, rolled their eyes with exasperation, or walked away in disgust.

We were great together and hated to spend time apart. Our love for each other was a lock around each our hearts, preventing us from letting go or allowing anyone else in. But we both tried anyway and failed.

That was me and my love from the moment we met. No matter how hard we tried to forget the other when the pain became too much to bear, we couldn't.

Once we chose each other despite all the reasons not to, everything changed. Loving each other through the good times became enough to get us through the bad ones.

He was the other half of me, in a way nobody else ever managed to become. We needed each other even when we couldn't stand to remain in the same room together.

We were poison—toxic. We were the disease and its cure. We fought against the inevitable—both with each other and against one another. Neither of us ever won a battle.

Of course, we never knew how much loving each other would change the course of everything. Or how much it would affect us for the rest of our lives either.

Nobody who saw me now would believe I loved him much at all. They would think me selfish for killing myself after he died... for taking away a second person they loved instead of only having to deal with one loss.

But they didn't know how much it hurt every inch of my body inside and out to not have him on this planet with me.

Some people make it back from the death of a loved one. Not me. I ached to take my last breath like an alcoholic who yearned for one more drink.

I would never breathe easy without him again.

And when the time came to move on like I knew he would want, it wouldn't happen. Not because my promises meant nothing, but because I needed him more than the world had or would ever have need of me. If there was a heaven, I would see him there; if there wasn't, then perhaps we would meet again in a new life.

Then again, even if nothing happened after I died? Even if death began the moment I drew my last breath of life and led to nothing else? Didn't matter because I would be dead and never have to experience the pain of missing him ever again.

No redemption for me. This wasn't the start of a love story, after all; it was the finale.

And the truth was that nobody could save me from the decision I made to end my life. The pain had increased with every passing moment since his death and was now at an unbearable level.

So, before I closed my eyes forever, I wanted to remember it all. The beginning, the middle, and the end. The good, the bad, the ugly. As well as the love-making that gripped my soul and lingered without remorse or regret long past its occurrence. The laughter, the tears, the fights, the making up, and the joy of living as well as the pain.

Because our romance hadn't ended when he took his last breath. The only happy ending to our story would be when I drew my last one as well and joined him six feet under.

CHAPTER 1
JULY 4TH

I met Banner St. James as a child for the first and only time when I was eight years old. We were both at a party attended by both our family and friends alike.

The adults sat around a table in the backyard — talking, sipping on their beers, and laughing. Meanwhile, the children ran around in their swimming gear. They jumped through the sprinkler and splashed in the kiddie pools, having fun even though it wasn't hot outside.

Except for me. I wore a bright blue one-piece bathing suit because my mom made me. Swimming or getting wet outside of bath time wasn't something I enjoyed, though. I didn't like it and instead, while they all played, I sat in the shade, my nose buried in a book.

The adults got the cookout started, and at five, they announced that the food was ready. I headed inside to use the bathroom.

Upon my return, almost all the kids waited in line with their parents to get something to eat.

That's when my eyes landed on him.

This boy sat in my chair — the one I had moved under the tree to use — and held my book in his hands. I hadn't seen him arrive, so I didn't know who he belonged to, even though he looked familiar.

All I knew was that he was rude to take my chair and even more rude for glaring at me as I approached him.

When I stopped in front of him, my legs almost touching his, I put both hands on my hips and scowled right back. "That's my chair."

His expression didn't change as he stood up. His action forced me to take a step back to avoid colliding as he turned toward the chair. Then he leaned in to stare at the plastic seat for a moment before facing me once again and sitting back down. "There's no name on it."

"That's stupid. Nobody puts their names on chairs. I've been sitting here all day."

"Prove it." He smiled, showcasing his slightly crooked teeth. My book remained tight in his grip as he crossed his arms over his chest. "I'll wait."

I pointed at my book as proof. "That's my book, too. I left it on the chair and you need to give both of them back."

"Or what? You'll tell on me?"

"No." Stepping forward again, I giggled and rested my hands on his bare knees, then glared at him. "If you don't give me back my book, I'll fall down and scream and say you pushed me."

He didn't react as I expected. Instead, he blinked, his grin widening as he leaned forward until our faces were inches apart. His blue eyes stared into mine as he said, "I'm Banner. Who are you?"

The moment he said his name I knew who he was. Glancing over at where our mothers stood together serving food, I knew now why he was being such a jerk. My hands left his knees as I straightened and held my hand out for my book as I said, "Valerie. And you can keep the chair. I just want my book back."

"Good." His smile disappeared as he held the book out to me, and after it was back in my hands, his expression soured. Crossing his arms again, he averted his gaze after mumbling, "See ya later, Valerie."

I didn't understand why he dismissed me that way, but my mother called out for me to come and eat before I could ask. Figuring I could ask him later, I mumbled back at him, "See ya," and then went to get some food.

LATER NEVER CAME.

Much to my mother's distress, Banner and his parents left not long after everyone finished eating. Their flight took off at nine that evening.

"Ten years since I've seen her, and she visits me only to tell me they are moving to London as soon as they can get to the airport!" My mother moaned to my father while washing the dishes several hours later as I swept the kitchen floor. "Who knows when we'll see them again?"

My father, always the one who chose to look at the positive side of things, wrapped his arm around my mother's waist. Hugging her close, he smiled down at her. "At least you're speaking again. A step in the right direction, isn't it?"

"Yes, I suppose it is." Finishing up, she washed her hands, turned the faucet off, and turned to me while drying them. "Valerie, I saw you talking to Banner. Last time I saw him, he was a little shy of three and such a rascal. He's a nice boy though, isn't he?"

Scooping the dirt onto the dustpan, I shrugged and walked over to the trash can without looking at them. "He wasn't mean, but he wasn't nice either. Stole my chair and my book when I went to the bathroom."

Both she and my father laughed for a second before she said, "Oh, honey. That's just boys for you. Judy said he's not happy about moving away from his friends and who can blame the poor boy? His whole life was in California, but he'll adjust."

I acknowledged what she said with a nod before they left the room. Beyond that, I didn't think much about it. I had more important things to do, such as read my book and find out who the villain was.

And although my mother had hoped they would remain in contact after the visit, they didn't.

Maybe if they had, things would have turned out differently.

But, because they didn't, it wasn't long before I forgot all about him.

CHAPTER 2

JANUARY 1ST

My birthday falling on the first of the year had always annoyed me.

Turned out that no longer held true, especially for my twenty-first birthday. I sat at a table in a rowdy club with my two best friends — Macy and Sarah. They made the evening worth it, especially as the clock struck midnight. That's when they yelled above the crowd, "Happy New Year and Happy Birthday!"

And then, seconds later, the three of us tipped back the shots Macy ordered. It wasn't the first time for me in general, just the first one in public, and when she suggested another I held up a hand.

"You know I've got a big day with my parents throwing a party, so I'll pass on having anything else to drink. Don't need a hangover." I smiled when they both whined, pointing to the dance floor to distract them. "But it doesn't mean we can't have fun. Let's go!"

We headed to the dance floor because we loved nothing more than having a good time, even if it didn't involve alcohol. The music seemed to blare louder on the floor, and it was packed with bodies, so we had to find our spot and stick with it. Before long, I was sweating and needed to use the restroom, so I pulled Macy aside to tell her, "I'll be right back. Going to the bathroom."

She nodded and yelled back, even though we were standing next to each other. "Want me to come with you?"

I shook my head, not wanting to yell again. She gave me a single thumbs-up before smiling and turning away to rejoin the group of guys we were dancing with.

I headed to the bathroom near the front of the club. Five minutes later, I stepped out into the hallway and walked right into a large, heated body.

"Damn," a man said, the deep sound of his lightly-accented voice making my stomach clench. His warm hands came up to grab my upper arms for a mere second before dropping away once I steadied on my heels. "Sorry."

"No problem." As I lifted my head to look up into his face, anything else I could have said died in my throat at the sight of him. He had a bright, straight smile and intense dark blue eyes that gazed down at me with unabashed interest.

I took in the rest of him. He was around five-ten with

shaggy brown hair and a clean-shaven face. Didn't hurt that he smelled enticing— subtle and sweet smelling, yet masculine. It made me want to lean in and sniff him, which is when I realized we were staring at each other mutely.

After a few moments, his expression changed to a weird mix of disappointment and concern when I stepped back.

"Are you all right?"

"Uh, yeah." I forced myself to blink and clear my throat before smiling. "I never literally run into people, so I think it scrambled my brain there for a minute."

"Scrambled...?" He laughed, his shoulders relaxing as he understood I made a joke. Slipping his hands into his jean pockets, it seemed as if he had all the time in the world to chat to me in this hallway. "Have we met before? You look familiar."

"No." My reply came out with a soft laugh. When his brows furrowed as if wondering why I found that funny, there was nothing for me to do except be honest since I couldn't find another way to explain. "I think I would remember meeting someone who looked like you."

His grin widened, his eyes sparking with interest as a blush took over my cheeks, and he nodded behind me. "I need some fresh air. Want to join me?"

Since there was a bouncer always standing outside to keep an eye on things, that meant we wouldn't be all alone. I nodded my agreement to indulge my sudden, extreme curiosity. "I'll be there in a minute. I have to let my friends know I'm going outside."

"Sure. I'll see you in a minute."

He turned and went to the door as I turned to head in the opposite direction.

What the hell was I doing? I had an insane urge to sniff a man I just met, then practically screamed how attractive I found him. And now I had agreed to go outside with him without thinking about it?

Then again, he thought he recognized me and maybe we had met before. Perhaps at a time where something more significant caused me to not recall the event?

Who knew.

Either way, I told Macy and Sarah I would be right outside getting some fresh air if they needed me. They both gave me two huge thumbs-up and went right back to dancing. Seemed they were enjoying themselves too much to wonder why I would go outside to stand in the cold by myself.

When I stepped out the door less than a minute later into the crisp night air — it was on the cusp of freezing but with zero breeze — the bouncer acknowledged me with a nod as the door clicked shut behind me. I didn't even get to turn my head to look for the guy before his voice rang out from the left.

"Over here." Turning, I saw him leaning against the building and he shrugged out of his jacket, holding it out to me with a smile as I approached. "You're going to need this."

"Thanks." I took the coat from his grip and slipping my arms into it, instantly surrounded by his smell and his warmth. "It was dumb of me not to grab mine from the coatroom."

"Nah. I'm hot anyway."

Yes, he was.

Crossing my arms over my chest as my cheeks flushed from the thought more than the cold, I leaned back against the building with a sigh. He propped himself with an elbow while facing my way.

"Something tells me you would say that just so I don't feel guilty about you freezing out here."

"You might be right," he admitted with a chuckle before his expression turned more thoughtful. "And I know you said we haven't met before, but are you sure?"

"I don't know. Cleveland's a pretty big area." I shrugged. "It's possible we've run into each other, though. Somewhere, somehow."

"Possibly. Do you gamble?"

"No. Why?"

"Because my company owns the newest casino downtown," he said with a laugh. "And I spend more time there than I should. My mother says I need to get a hobby, while my father tells her to be grateful I'm not a delinquent."

I smiled at that before making sure I heard him correctly. "The newest casino? As in, you own the Crystal?" I shook my head in disbelief as he nodded in reply. "Wow. My friends have gone there a few times since it opened last year. Even if I had been old enough to go, I have terrible luck, so I wouldn't have put myself in a position to lose money quickly."

He quirked a brow and cleared his throat, his expression a bit sheepish as he asked, "How old are you?"

"Twenty-one." I lifted my arm to look at my watch. "As of an hour and thirty minutes ago."

"Well, happy birthday."

"Thanks. I had you worried there for a second, didn't I?"

Shaking his head, he chuckled and straightened away from the wall. Keeping his gaze locked on mine, he held out his hand in introduction. "Guess we haven't met before, then, because I would've been stupid not to remember you. I'm Brad."

Taking his hand, I almost wanted to break my rule about not giving out my real name when meeting men in bars or clubs. Then again, perhaps it was best not to even if he wasn't exaggerating about his identity. "Anne."

He squeezed my hand and smirked. "You don't look like an Anne."

I didn't know how one looked like a name and shot back at him. "You don't look like a Brad."

With another laugh, he released my hand and asked, "How about you? Are you in college?"

"Yes." Tingling from the contact, I clenched my hand into a fist and slipped it behind my back, forcing myself to focus on the conversation rather than the odd way he made me feel. "I'm a junior at Cleveland State. Double major in International Relations and French."

"Impressive. I bet that keeps you quite busy."

"Yeah, it does, but not enough I don't find time to have fun." I tilted my head toward the club's front doors. "Even before I could drink, this was one of my favorite places to come to on a Friday night."

"Nice. Tonight is a first for me. Not much of a club goer and never have been."

"And you're wasting your experience by standing outside in the cold with me?"

"No." He stepped a bit closer and put his right hand flat against the wall, making it so we nearly touched but I could escape if necessary. "I was about to leave from excessive boredom when we bumped into each other and you made the comment about our collision scrambling your brain."

I couldn't help but smile at that. "I suppose that was a funny thing to say."

"Yes, it was." He leaned in until I had to lift my chin to look into his eyes and lowered his voice. "I have a question for you and need your complete honesty."

"I'm always honest."

"Good." His eyes flicked to my mouth and back up to my eyes as he turned all serious. "Did you feel the instant and intense attraction between us in that hallway or was it just me?"

My stomach flipped at his question even though I knew it was coming. Instead of giving a straight 'yes' answer because I didn't know what to do about the draw between us, I relaxed the hand at my side and whispered my response. "My hand still tingles from where you held it, if that tells you anything."

"It tells me everything I need to know. Enough to do this."

That's all he said before moving the rest of the way in, his hand on the wall moving to the back of my neck. His other arm wrapped around my waist as he covered my mouth with his warm-despite-the-outside-temperature lips.

My hands landed on his chest and clung to the soft fabric of his white button-down shirt as he coaxed my mouth open. Then, he slipped his tongue inside with the ease of a man who knew how to get what he wanted. When his tongue tangled with mine, the earlier excitement that caused my stomach to flip dispersed throughout my entire body. I had never experienced this before in my life, every inch of me electrified and begging for more.

I had an inexplicable desire to get closer while also running in the opposite direction. When I whimpered into his mouth as he tugged me closer, he released a tortured groan before pulling away. "Holy fuck."

My shaking legs and pounding heart agreed with his sentiment, because it showed the kiss affected him as much as it had me. It was clear neither of us had thought we would experience that.

I didn't know what to say or what to do. Before I could figure out either, the sound of someone howling while retching nearby penetrated the little bubble around us. How could one moment make me question my decision to avoid relationships while in school?

He stepped back when I pushed at him with my hands and turned to look for who interrupted our moment at the same time as I did.

Macy and Sarah stood together near the curb with a waiting taxi, both wobbling on their feet. Macy gave a wild wave of her hand in my direction as she slurred, "Hey girl, we need to go!"

I acknowledged her with a wave of my own, then glanced at Brad to find him staring at me with a smile on his lips and his hands back in his pockets. I still didn't know what to say. It wasn't like we had time to say much with my friends climbing into the cab, so I kept things simple. "They need me, so I've got to go."

"Of course." He looked over at my friends and then back at me before leaning in with a definite gleam in his eyes. "I would love to take you out sometime. You know where to find me if you decide to take me up on the offer."

He turned and walked away without waiting for a reply. I was left staring at him with lips that would never forget the kiss he had bestowed upon them. That is, until Macy called out again. "Come on, before she gets more sick!"

I turned and walked to the taxi in a daze. It wasn't until I was packed inside with Macy and Sarah on our way home that I realized he walked away without his jacket. And despite all the reasons I shouldn't, this gave me the perfect excuse to see him again.

To see if tonight had been a fluke or something more.

CHAPTER 3

"Did you have a nice night out with your friends?" My mom asked me after I finally walked into the kitchen at nine AM. Turning to face me with an egg-covered spatula in one hand, she was happy as always and smiling. "And are you hungry?"

"I'm starving." Covering my mouth to yawn, I retrieved a glass from the cupboard and walked to the fridge. "And yeah, it was fun."

"Good." She turned back to the stove and continued to cook, humming the whole time as I filled my glass with orange juice. When I stepped up next to her to see if she wanted help, she shooed me away with a cluck of her tongue. "It's your birthday. Go sit down and it will be ready soon."

"Okay, okay."

On a typical day I would insist, and she would give in,

but not today. I knew from past years that she refused to let me help on my birthday no matter how much she knew I liked to cook.

Both of my parents were pretty great. I was the youngest child as well as their only daughter. I had twin brothers, Colin and Timothy, who were four years older than me. My parents spoiled us as much as they could. They also taught us the value of hard work and how to pull our weight at home since the day we were born.

Well, all right, maybe three or four years after that.

I respected and loved them. When they asked me to live at home upon my decision to attend Cleveland State, I didn't hesitate to agree. In truth, I wanted to live on-campus, but they were paying for my schooling as they had for my brothers. There weren't any non-selfish reasons to move out, so at home I would stay until graduation.

It had worked out well until this point. Nothing seemed likely to change because I respected their rules and they treated me as the adult they had a hand in me becoming.

My father walked in as my mother placed the food in the center of the table. After pressing a kiss to her lips as they sat down next to each other, he smiled at me with a pointed glance at my cup. "Morning, sweetheart. Not hungover, are you?"

"No, Dad. I only had one drink." I laughed while

scooping some eggs onto my place. "I knew better than to get drunk when you guys are throwing a party."

"We're that predictable, are we?"

I didn't answer because yes, they were, and we all ate our breakfast in relative silence.

Soon after my parents reminded me that the party would start at two this afternoon and I better not be late. It was a dual birthday and New Year's Day party they'd thrown every year since I turned fourteen. That meant most people who were going to attend didn't drink much, if at all, the evening before.

The time gave me a few hours to do some things for myself. So, I returned to my room and caught sight of the jacket from last night hanging on the chair in my room. Turning on my computer, I searched for the number to call whatever-his-name was to return it.

Didn't take me long to locate a number to the casino, although I didn't see his name anywhere any of the pages. I guess when it came to a casino such information really didn't matter.

Pulling out my iPhone from my purse, I dialed the number. It barely rang once before a lady with a super sweet and annoying voice answered. "Crystal Casino, this is Jenny. How may I help you?"

Shit.

I had no idea what his real name was and I wasn't going to ask for the owner of the casino in case the guy had lied. Feeling stupid, I hung up after mumbling, "Sorry, wrong number."

Guess I would have to go up there and find him on my own to give him his jacket back, if what he said was true. With that, I went over to my dresser, grabbed something to wear, and headed to get a shower.

AFTER COLLECTING MY COAT FROM THE CLUB, I arrived at the casino a few minutes before noon. The man near the doors checked my ID and the benefit of being twenty-one as of today couldn't be better since I wouldn't have been able to enter otherwise.

I smiled at him, walked a few steps, then whirled around and pointed at the jacket slung over my arm as I said, "I'm looking for the owner. This is his jacket and I need to return it."

"Sure, it is, honey." He laughed and dismissed me by turning back to the line of people waiting for him to check their I.D.'s.

Okay then, I would have to find someone else to direct me to the correct place. No doubt in my mind that he had an office in this casino or something like it.

Turned out, I didn't need anyone's help because as I strolled past the rows of machines, there he was talking to another man around his age. Both wore black suits with white shirts and black ties, and they headed right in my direction.

I stopped abruptly in the middle of the aisle and someone bumped my arm as they walked by, looking back to glare at me before continuing on their way.

His friend noticed me first, nudging the object of my attention in his side, who then grinned with pure pleasure as his eyes met mine. He said something to his friend as they approached . As he halted in front of me, his friend winked at him, slapped him the shoulder, and said in a thick (maybe British?) accent, "See you later, bro." Then he walked past us without saying anything to me.

"My business partner, Sam." He flicked his gaze toward his jacket as I held it out to him silently. "Did you come all this way just to give that back?"

"Well, it isn't mine. And coming here wasn't that far."

He took it from my grasp with one hand and rubbed his lip with the pad of his thumb on the other. The movement brought my attention to his mouth. He smirked when he noticed, dropping his hand as he stepped closer until we were less than six inches apart. "Join me for lunch."

Even though his invitation was more demand than request, I didn't hesitate to respond. "I'd like that, Brad."

His eyes flashed with laughter and another emotion I didn't dare analyze. "As would I, Anne."

Still playing that game, were we? All right, I would be

Anne for the afternoon — not that it was a straight up lie, being my middle name.

"This way," he said after a moment where I thought maybe he waited for me to tell him my real name. Then he offered his arm for me to take and gave a short bob of his head in the direction he had just came from. "No need to leave when we have amazing food."

"Do you? As the owner, are you really permitted to say anything except how great this place is?"

"No." We both laughed as he led the way once I hooked my arm around his and then he flashed his beautiful smile my way once again. "But once you're here for a bit and have sampled the food, I'm positive you'll believe it as much as I do."

"I'm sure."

The sign of the indoor restaurant came into sight right as my phone buzzed in my pocket. I pulled it out of my pocket and saw a text from my mother, requesting my presence at home immediately.

"Crap."

He stopped, his mouth frowning even as his eyes twinkled with good humor. "Have to go already? I didn't even get the chance to scare you away with my bad table manners."

I liked how he wasn't put off by my sudden need to leave after coming all this way. "Yes, I'm sorry. My mother needs me and we're having a party later so—"

"Hey, no problem." He moved his arm, sliding his hand down until it clasped mine, and then brought it to his mouth to kiss the back of it. "Raincheck?"

My lips parted, mouth suddenly parched at his touch, a reminder of the intoxicating and intense kiss we shared last night. The rapid darkening of his eyes and tighter grip on my hand gave away his awareness of my desire and declared his own hadn't diminished since then either.

I wanted him, he wanted me, and neither of us were trying to hide it.

He leaned in when I didn't answer, gripping my hand tighter as he whispered in my ear, "Give me five minutes."

Five more minutes for what, I didn't know and didn't care. No matter that we met barely more than twelve hours ago; I wouldn't deny his request because I wanted him to touch me as badly as he wanted to do it.

When I gave my consent with a silent nod, he dragged me away from the restaurant, then led us down a long hallway.

It wasn't as well-lit and took me away from anyone who might hear me scream in case he was a murderer. Yet, when he opened a door that led to a room filled with tables and chairs, I knew his decision to bring us here would do us both a favor.

Once inside the room, he tossed the coat on the floor. Backing me up against the door with zero hesitation, he covered my lips with his. The kiss wasn't anything like the one from last night.

No, this one blew the other away. He ravaged my mouth with his lips and tongue while I mindlessly gripped his shoulders. Feeling his arousal against right where I would want him if we were naked, I bucked my hips to rub against his hardness so there would be no questions about how badly I wanted more. Also to let him know I wouldn't stop him if he wanted to go further, too.

Who cared if our first time was a quickie when it had this much fire?

He must've had the same thought. His hands slipped between our bodies seconds later as he unbuttoned my jeans. I felt him tug them down because of how tight they were. I thought he would break the kiss to at least make me step out of one leg, but no. He simply slid one hand inside my panties and between my legs.

One finger, then two, were roughly shoved inside me, but it didn't hurt because my body was more than prepared for him. For this.

My gasp and moans were trapped inside his mouth. He chuckled as my nails dug into his skin through the fabric of his suit jacket, my lower body rolling with the thrust of his fingers.

Overtaken by the need to use his hand to get off before heading home, something I knew would please him, I arched into his touch with pleasure. I didn't know why it mattered when I could do this myself. There was something about the way his strong body kept me locked in place while his hand works its magic that turned me on in an entirely new way.

When the orgasm hit, my whole body stiffened with a jolt before shaking with the release and I cried out into his mouth.

With our mouths still connected, I felt the curve of his lips against mine as he began to draw away completely, including the removal of his hand from my body. He buttoned my pants as I held onto his shoulders to remain steady, my whole body humming with pleasure from the inside out.

The silence should've been awkward, yet it wasn't.

Instead, at the sound of phone chirping with another message, my arms slipped away from his shoulders rather unwillingly. My sigh was heavy at having such a perfect moment ending way too quick.

"Let me give you my number," he said when I reached into my pocket to grab my phone all while my body remained flushed from his attention. "We'll do dinner."

I liked the way he didn't ask. Then again, after how I let him get me off inside his casino, what were the chances of me saying no?

"Okay." I met his gaze, opened up a new contact on my phone, and smiled. "What is it?"

His eyes were on my lips the entire time he told me his

number, one slow digit at a time. He laughed when his phone went off seconds after he finished.

"That's me." He knew but I told him anyway because he didn't reach for his phone. Definitely liked how he gave me his undivided attention. "Talk later?"

"Any time."

Stepping closer, he captured my lips in a slow, sensual kiss that made me wish I didn't have to leave. He ended it before I could decide to ignore my mother's summons for the diversion of a man I wanted to get to know better.

Then, he walked me to the front doors of the casino, reiterated his invitation for dinner once more, and left me to go home with tingling lips that kept me distracted for hours afterward.

"Busy?"

Ugh. My second message to him since he gave me his number two weeks ago and it sucked.

I thought he would text me back again by now. Other than the one time two days after I returned his coat where he responded with, "Sorry, I can't talk right now," he hadn't said anything else.

Well, I didn't plan on waiting around. Not really.

All right. He might have more time than I would give anyone else because what happened in the room that day had thrown me for a loop. However, it would be nice if he sent me another message, even one simply telling me everything's fine. That he would text me soon.

This silence ticked me off way more than it should. That's how I knew it was time to stop waiting for him to contact me again, even as I looked at my phone just one more time.

"Val, why the hell do you keep checking your phone?" Macy laughed and leaned into my side. She was already pretty wasted even though it was midnight and we'd only been there an hour. "Are me and Sarah that boring?"

Feeling bad, I set my phone on the table face down and put my arm around her shoulders. "Sorry."

"No, no." Macy arched her brows and wiggled them suggestively. "Is it that guy we saw you with on your birthday? Because if it is, we understand. He was hot."

It took me a moment to register her remembering him in spite of how drunk they both were, especially since they hadn't said anything until just now. "Uh, yeah, actually."

She must've expected me to say no because her eyes rounded while Sarah squealed and said, "Tell us everything!"

So, I did even though there wasn't much to tell. By the time I got to the part at the casino they both stared at me with their mouths hanging open.

Macy spoke first, voice incredulous. "You let him do what?"

"Val." Sarah, always the one concerned about people's feelings, reached across the table to cover my hand. "Seriously, you guys haven't talked, and he only responded to your text once? That's bullshit."

It was, but I refused to see him in a bad light just because he hasn't texted me again. We barely knew each other. I got it, I truly did, even if it totally blew with happening this way.

"We really hit it off, guys." When they both gave me a skeptical look, I hated how my eyes teared up and closed them to try to stop them from falling. "I don't know. I want to give him the benefit of the doubt. Maybe something happened."

"Maybe," they mumbled, skeptical and almost in unison.

I heard their uncertainty. Which was a lot more solid along with going in a completely different direction than mine.

When he didn't respond to my message by the time we headed home in a taxi a little more than hours later, I became so determined to forget whatever went on between us that I deleted his number.

Also made a promise to myself not to listen to his excuses if or when he ever decided to contact me.

Turned out it would be way worse when the moment finally arrived.

My reaction wasn't one anyone who knew me would ever expect, least of all myself.

I woke in the morning with one hell of a hangover and still no message.

Rolling over, the time on the clock — two after eleven – made me groan. I didn't want to get out of bed even as I sat up, swung my legs to the edge, and stood up before the warmth could entice me back in for the rest of the day.

Grabbing a change of clothes, I headed down the hall to get a shower, turning my music up on my phone once inside. The night out, along with the time I spent crying like an idiot, had me feeling like crap. I used the hot water to wash it all away because there wasn't anything else to do except get over it and move on.

I didn't need the complication of a relationship anyway. Although I had one in high school for a couple years, that ended my junior year shortly after he'd taken my virginity. Nobody had interested me since then.

Well, until I met him.

Upon stepping out of the shower, I heard the front door shut downstairs and rushed to get dressed. My parents hadn't mentioned any company today; just in case, I didn't want them to think I forgot even if that were the truth.

Running down the steps, I walked toward the living room, only to halt in the doorway at the sight of my mother sitting on the couch. My father had her wrapped in his arms while she sobbed her eyes out.

The words, "What's wrong?" shot out of my mouth before I registered there were other people in the room.

Judy sat on the love seat across from my parents, tears streaming down her cheeks. Her husband was nowhere in sight.

In that moment, nobody had to say anything. I knew instinctively he wouldn't be arriving at all. That could be the only explanation for her being here, and for the tears, because she never went anywhere without him. She followed that man around the world with no regard to what damage it did to her relationship with my mother.

And that's why she came back. Without her husband, the man who had been my mother's best friend all through childhood before they ended up marrying instead, she had her son and us.

The son who now stood at the window, staring out into our yard where the snow poured down with his hands inside his suit pockets. He turned so slowly at my question that my heart broke piece-by-piece as his face came into view.

He knew before I came downstairs. How could he not, with all the pictures my proud parents had placed around the house of me and my brothers? He'd had time to prepare, to show nothing on his face while his dark blue eyes swirled with apology and banked emotions.

But there had been no warning of the ugly truth for me.

Brad, the man who had gotten me off with his hand two weeks ago, was Banner.

Banner, my aunt Judy's son.

My fucking first cousin.

A million indiscernible thoughts and feelings swirled around in my head as my entire world focused on him. My entire body went lax as the shock of it all spread throughout, heart clenching as the realization stole my breath.

I heard my father say something that failed to penetrate the fog around me. Failed to break the connection of my gaze and Banner's. And the way the sight of him turned me on didn't dissipate despite the new information slamming into my brain.

How fucked up did that make me?

My stomach roiled, threatening to get rid of the alcohol from last night because there wasn't anything else in it.

Both of my hands came up to my mouth as the threat turned into reality, giving me the perfect opportunity to run away.

Once inside the safety of the bathroom, my feelings found a new way to exit my body besides tears.

I WASN'T IN THE BATHROOM LONG BEFORE A KNOCK came at the door.

Having finished throwing up the alcohol, I brushed my teeth as well as my tongue. Standing frozen while staring into the mirror, I wondered how the hell I could walk out of here with my head held high.

Sure, I hadn't known, and neither had he, but still. And it should have immediately shut down the attraction, yet it hadn't for me, which was the worst of all.

How could I have missed it? Why hadn't I been more cautious as I had been with other guys? Asked more questions? Of course, the answer is shameful. My attraction had been so strong I failed to notice the strong resemblance to his mother, who looked a lot like my own.

With no idea what to do or say if I had to face them, I remained standing there silently, ignoring the knock at the door. Whoever it was, I wanted them to go away and leave me alone.

But that would be too easy because of all the people who could've come after me, of course Banner was it.

"Valerie." He jiggled the door handle when I didn't respond, his frustrated sigh coming through loud and clear. "Let me in unless you want our parents to hear this conversation."

The moment I clicked the lock, the door opened. He came in while I backed up further inside the bathroom to avoid touching him. After enclosing us inside, he faced me while slipping his hands into his pockets. He was large and out of place in our tiny bathroom, and neither of us seemed inclined to talk first.

Finally, as he stared at with me all the emotions in his eyes that swirled around in my chest, I couldn't take it any longer and whispered, "What the hell, Banner?"

"I told you to call me Brad," he replied with laughter in his eyes. His smile dimmed a little when I glared but the light in his gaze didn't as he explained. "Bradford is my middle name, but everyone merely calls me Brad. Banner disappeared a long time ago; I didn't like it."

"Ah. That makes sense." It did, even though I wasn't breathing any easier because of it, and I teased him to remind us both of who we were. "Banner Bradford St. James. That's a mouthful."

He smirked. "That's what I told my parents when I was sixteen and requested everyone call me Brad."

"I've always thought of you as Banner, the jerk who stole my chair and book."

Grinning, he removed his hands from his pockets and stepped closer. When he rested them on my shoulders, my breath almost stopped in the process. "And you're not Anne. You're Valerie, the girl who threatened to fall down, then blame it on me."

I should've laughed at his retort. Plus he remembered that day as well as I did, but the only thing running through my mind was his proximity to me. Too close. Too intimate.

Our mutual attraction wasn't hidden in this bathroom. Every emotion I currently experienced was written all over my face while his closeness demonstrated how much he wanted me despite our new reality.

"This is fucked up." I closed my eyes because not looking at him made it easier to be brutally honest like we needed to in this moment. "We're fucked up."

"No, we're not." He kissed my temple. One of his arms wrapped around my lower back while the other placed my head in the crook of his shoulder and stroked my hair. "We didn't know."

With no idea of how he could remain so calm through all this, I asked the question we both wondered about now. "And now that we do?"

"We'll talk more about that later," he muttered into the top of my head. "For now, we should head back downstairs before one of them decide to check on us."

He was right. To our families, we had only met once as children. Catching us together and hugging would raise questions neither of us were ready to answer.

So, I pulled away first, only to open my eyes as he lowered his head toward mine. His hand slid up from my back to behind my neck as he muttered, "Shit."

It was an accurate description of the trouble we were in as our lips met in a soft, sweet kiss. It didn't last long yet confirmed this wasn't going to end today no matter how much it should.

Then, when we separated, I said something I should've told him the moment he walked into the bathroom. "I'm sorry about your dad."

Stepping back, he grabbed my hand. "Me too."

He looked back at me while opening the door, getting a grip on his desire for me enough to allow the grief to show once more on his face. Then, he squeezed my hand tighter instead of saying anything else as he led the way back downstairs.

Our deception began the moment our hands parted when we neared the living room where our parents waited. Neither of us were aware of how the idea of us would change everyone's lives one day.

WITH NOTHING TO DO FOR THE DAY, I HEADED straight to the casino to surprise Banner.

He and his mother stayed for dinner with us the other night, which is when I learned his father had a heart attack a few hours after I returned his coat. It explained everything as he had left the next morning to join his parents in London after his mother called him, where his father died from congestive heart failure a mere two days after his arrival.

If I were him, I wouldn't have worried about messaging me at all in the middle of such a crisis, let alone the one time he did. So, I'm grateful he took the time to respond that once, even if it left me clueless as to what really went on.

And after they left my house, he called me about an hour later. We spent the whole night talking about everything except the one important thing between us we shouldn't ignore.

We avoided discussing it because we didn't have to face the music that way. In general, first cousins being together was a pairing most looked down upon. Although I didn't ask his thoughts, the chance our family would approve seemed unlikely to me.

I knew for sure because after we got off the phone the first evening, my curiosity led me to search the internet for any laws about it. I found them without too much effort. It wasn't hard — more like totally disheartening.

In some states, the relationship is not permitted, but not in Ohio. No, if we ever wanted to, we could live together or have children, yet marriage was out of the question. What kind of sense was that, to allow that but not the other?

Then again, not much of this whole thing made sense. There have been moments where I wondered why the hell I hadn't ended things right there in that bathroom. Or why he hadn't, for that matter.

We had an intense attraction, yes. However, we barely knew each other and weren't in love. I couldn't help but wonder what was the right thing to do. Should we put a stop to this whole thing before we got to that point? Or was giving us a shot to see if there truly was anything the better thing to do instead of always wondering?

Incredibly difficult for me to answer, as I had no one to

ask since I needed to do this on my own. I didn't believe anyone would understand why we continued seeing each other after becoming aware of our familial connection... not even my best friends.

Yet, I didn't want to keep secrets. Eventually I would have to say something if things worked out; for now I was happy to keep this between the two of us.

As I arrived at the casino and had my ID checked, I couldn't resist smiling at how my refusing to call him Brad didn't seem to bother him. Or maybe he realized correcting me every time wouldn't work so he gave up after the second try.

Putting my ID back in my purse, I walked toward the rear of the casino and the elevator Banner told me would take me up to his office. On the way up, I reapplied my lip gloss and ran my hands through my hair, blowing a kiss and winking at the camera in the corner as it came to a stop.

With any fantasies I might've had involving Banner and the elevator murdered by the presence of the camera, I stepped off and headed to the right. I didn't know if he would be in his office, but he did tell me he never left before nine in the evening so being only four pm made arriving unannounced a safe bet.

Discovering his door closed, I tapped on it lightly and received a response almost instantly.

"Come in." He didn't even look up when I opened the

door, stepped inside, and shut it behind me so we had some privacy. "What is it?"

"I think you meant who." My statement along with my laughter brought his head shooting up, his hand pausing in whatever he was writing as I said, "Probably should question who is at your door before you tell anyone to just come on in."

"No need as there isn't much to worry about," he assured me with a suggestive wink as he tossed the pen and leaned back in his chair. "Every inch of this casino is monitored apart from two rooms only accessible to Sam and myself."

Flushing as his wink told me we had used one of those rooms, I set down my messenger bag and purse off to the side of the door, then walked toward him. "I hope it's okay I just dropped by."

"Absolutely. In fact," he said with a crook of his finger encouraging me to move closer, "I planned on messaging to ask if you were free tonight."

"What, no call?" I stopped next to his desk, hands on my hips as I quirked a brow. "And do you usually ask a girl out on a date with such short notice?"

"Who says it's a date?" He chuckled at my frown, obviously messing with me, and moved until he faced me in his chair before tapping his leg. "Take a seat."

My mouth went dry and my heart tripped over itself in an instant. "On your lap?"

I expected him to tease me or tell me he was joking. He didn't, his gaze unwavering as he replied with a simple and guttural, "Yes."

A big part of me wanted to. A smaller bit saw this as another moment where we would step farther than we could return from before things went too far, and my expression gave away my indecision.

"You came here of your own accord," he said softly, understanding the fight going on within me, perhaps because he fought the same battle. "You're as intrigued as I am."

"I am." Dropping my arms to my sides, I licked my lips and took a hesitant step closer. "But, that's the thing. Shouldn't I be disgusted? We're family."

"The American view is antiquated, based on faulty genetic rationale. Many believe it will lead to genetic defects in any children born, but the risk is only four percent compared to two percent for non-related couples. Yes, I looked things up, as I'm sure you did." He smiled when I laughed and tapped his lap once more in invitation. "This isn't an issue in most other countries, such as England, where I lived until two years ago. Plus, I don't think of you as my cousin, Val. We met once. You were eight; I was thirteen. It isn't as if we grew up together."

My lips flattened because even though I didn't think of him as family either, the stories I read after finding out of others in the same situation and the reaction of their loved ones made my stomach churn with uncertainty. "What about our families?"

"What about them?" Rolling his chair toward me, he snatched one of my hands in his and tugged me down. Wrapping an arm around my waist to keep me from jumping up, he placed a light kiss on my cheek. "Relax, Val. We don't have to figure everything out today."

"I know."

"Do you?" As I softened in his hold, he re-positioned me to face him while straddling his lap, and grinned as he skimmed along the hem of my skirt with his warm hands. "Did you wear this short thing around all day? Isn't it freezing outside?"

"I did." His touch induced goosebumps on my legs and I covered his hands to stop them from moving. "And yes, it's like thirty-five, but it's not like it's snowing."

"As I haven't a clue how you manage in such a skimpy thing when it's cold like this, I shall take your word for it." His face inched toward mine, the luscious and subtle scent of his cologne teasing my senses, while his mouth slowly teased my lips with a soft, sweet kiss.

When I whispered his name, lifted my arms to slip them around his neck and scooted closer, he chuckled against my mouth. "You should know, I've decided sound of my name on your lips is incredibly sexy."

"Oh, really?"

"I wouldn't lie about that."

"Good to know." I laughed and shook my head, withdrawing a bit to gaze into his eyes. "What would you lie about?"

"Nothing." He quirked a brow, as if he found my question absurd. "I don't do lies. They're unnecessary and a waste of everyone's time. Wouldn't you agree?"

"Yeah, I think I do."

"You think?"

"Fine." I sighed. "I do agree. And I'm not good with lies, honestly. It's too hard to keep your story straight. Better to tell the truth and take whatever comes after it."

Maybe he saw something on my face, or in my expression, because his own softened as he once again cupped my face in his hands and pressed a gentle kiss on my lips. The touch was more comforting than sexual and when I sighed, our breaths mingled as he said, "We'll find a way to tell them, but not yet. Let's get to know each other more."

"I think that's a good idea."

"As do I, because the second we ran into each other in that club, the desire to kiss you was merely the beginning of what I'm positive will become more. Much more. Something I want to keep to myself for a little while longer."

Neither of us said anything for a while after that as his lips met mine once again, with a lot more passion and heat. By the time I headed home to get ready for our date in a few hours, I wasn't sure of anything other than I wanted his hands on me again by the end of the evening.

I should have thought with my head instead of letting my heart lead the way. But that's what happens when you're young and in the throes of what is none other than a tempest of emotions you can't ignore. Not even when it might be better to heed the warnings attempting to gain your attention.

Because, in the end, there wasn't any chance either of us would escape paying for our mutual refusal to walk away while we still could.

CHAPTER 6

"Oh! What are you doing here, Banner?"

Seemed I wasn't the only one who refused to call him by his preferred name. My mother pulled him into a hug before he could answer. Then she stepped back, fresh tears pricking her eyes as she glanced over her shoulder at me. "Are you two going somewhere?"

"Yeah, um..." Pausing to try and come up with a good reason for him showing up at our house, I licked my lips. My eyes flicked to his, where he smirked from his position in the doorway. Then they widened at the sight of flowers in his hands and my breath caught in my throat. Why had he thought it a good idea to bring me something like that when we were trying to keep us a secret for a while? "Um...well, you see..."

Banner must have seen my panic because he cleared his throat and caught my mother's attention, who turned back to him with a smile. "These are for you, Aunt Rose. And I thought, if you didn't mind, it would be nice to spend a little time with Valerie this evening. Figured we should get to know each since we're all living close to one another now."

"Well, you're a charmer like your father, aren't you?" My mother giggled and took the flowers, sniffing them before turning to me, her cheeks rosy. "You should've said something, honey. Of course, you two should go and have a good time. But don't stay out too late."

"Thank, Mom." I smiled and grabbed my coat from the nearby rack, slipping into it as she walked away from the door. "And you know there's nothing in the world that will make me stay out too late when I've got to get up at six in the morning."

"True." She waved goodbye and sniffed the flowers again. "Well, go on. Don't let me keep you any longer."

I kissed her on the cheek and stepped outside, shutting the door behind me. That's when Banner finally checked me out, his gaze sliding down my body slowly before making its way back up.

He held out a hand for me to take and grinned. "Ready for the surprise?"

"Um, sure." That's when I noticed he still wore his suit from work. "What exactly do you have planned for us? And am I not dressed up enough?"

"You're perfect."

Anybody else, I wouldn't have believed them. With Banner? The glint in his eye told me he meant it and my cheeks flushed at the compliment. "Thanks."

He led the way to his car, opened the door, and waited until I buckled my seat belt before shutting it. Then, he slid in on his side, slipped the key into the ignition, and backed out of the driveway.

Neither of us said anything more until we were at the first stoplight. That's when he leaned across the center to give me a long, hot kiss; one which left us both panting when he drew away.

"Couldn't wait any longer." He winked and focused on the road again as the light turned green. "What time do you want to be home by?"

"Midnight, at the latest."

"Ah, perfect then."

"Is it?" When he didn't answer, I reached over and covered his hand with mine, giving it a light squeeze, at which point he quirked a brow in my direction. "Tell me where we're going and why midnight is perfect."

"Because I haven't wasted money on tickets for tonight's performance at Severance Hall."

"I thought the Cleveland Orchestra went on strike?"

He shook his head and freed his hand from where it rested beneath mine to turn a particularly sharp corner. "They're threatening to as of the eighteenth if they can't reach some sort of compromise. Understandable considering they're playing without contracts right now, since August I believe."

"Really? Damn. I would be pissed and protesting, too."

"Exactly. But they aren't yet, so we're going to see them play tonight."

"Hey, I'm sure they appreciate the support. Let's hope everyone gets the terms they can live with. We all know nobody ever gets exactly what they want when it comes to the point of striking."

"Right."

"Did you know my parents used to take us kids to see the orchestra once a year when we were growing up?"

"I didn't, but I'm glad you're pleased we're going."

"Me, too."

He snatched my hand this time, bringing the back to his mouth in a sweet kiss as we finally approached Severance Hall. We found a place to park and walked to the entrance, holding hands the entire way. Even once we found our seats, he said he would only let go if I wanted him to.

I didn't.

The entire performance was amazing, the music beautiful. It had been a while since I came to watch the orchestra play, but they always did a terrific job. Tonight, they played Strauss's "Don Juan," Brahms' Symphony No. 2 and the Ades Violin Concerto.

The entire performance was captivating. Quite a few

times, I caught Banner staring at me instead of watching. But I suppose when it's the orchestra, all anyone really had to do was listen. Occasionally, he would lean in and nuzzle my neck, making me shiver and him chuckle softly into my ear.

By the end, I had thoroughly enjoyed our evening out, I was ready to go home. Morning would arrive before I was ready if I didn't get enough sleep.

The car ride back to my house was relatively quiet. I must have passed out for a few moments because my eyes opened to find the car shut off. Banner was crouching down on the curb next to my open door, his hand resting on my upper arm as he tried to wake me gently.

"Hey."

"Hey."

If his greeting was low, mine was almost a whisper, and we both smiled at each other simultaneously.

"You have the cutest little snore; did you know that?"

"Ugh." I rolled my eyes and unbuckled my seat belt. "Why would you tell me that? I'm a lady, I don't snore."

"I love it."

"Stop." Even though that word came out, I laughed and got out of the car as soon as he rose to his full height, slipping his hands into his pockets. After making sure to grab my purse, I shut the car door and took a slow, deep breath. "Tonight was great. Thank you for inviting me."

"It was my pleasure."

He stared at me while the cold wind blew his hair around, as well as mine, and I could tell this wasn't the way he wanted to say goodnight to the other. Same for me. But, we were in front of the house and the street lights were far too bright for us to risk even a single kiss. Although it wasn't likely my parents were still awake, I didn't want to take a chance no matter how much my lips ached to touch his.

"I'll text you after my class is over on Tuesday," I promised him, taking a step back. "Right after. Maybe we can do something then?"

"Absolutely."

"Night, Banner."

"Goodnight, Val. Sweet dreams."

"You, too."

He nodded, I pivoted on my heels and took the few steps toward the front door. I enjoyed the fact he watched me until I went inside, the cold shut out with nothing more than a tiny click of the latch behind me.

My dreams that evening involved the beautiful sound of music and Banner's gorgeous gaze drinking in every inch of my body as we laid in bed together.

The next morning, there was an alarming tightness in my chest. And it wouldn't go away, no matter how much I tried to convince myself there wasn't anything to worry about.

"You should stay the night."

Banner said the words softly as I laid in his bed, dressed only in my white lace bra and panties, while he rested on my left side, using his elbow to prop himself up so he could stare down at me.

Six days since our date night to see the orchestra and we hadn't done anything more than kiss with a little undressing and a few teasing caresses. Which surprised me, honestly, considering the way he had pushed me against the wall in the casino and got me off with his hand in speedy fashion.

I guess that was understandable, though.

Things had changed. And whether either of us admitted it out loud, we hesitated to take things between us any further than we already had. We could only go so far before there wouldn't be any turning back.

Before we couldn't pretend this wasn't serious or real and we would have to tell our families, which meant dealing with whatever that might entail for the both of us.

"Val? Are you going to stay?"

Not realizing I hadn't answered him, my cheeks bloomed with heat, and I shook my head. "I don't think that's a good idea."

"Why not?" When I didn't respond, he smiled. "I know you're worried about your mom. Just tell her you're staying with a friend. No need to give details. That way you aren't lying."

"I'm already lying by omission."

He scoffed at that. "Come on. You're not the only adult to have a relationship they aren't fully open about with their parents. Some things are just better left unsaid."

Exactly what I had a problem with.

"See?" I sat up and scooted until my back hit the headboard, glaring at him. "What are we doing, Banner? We both know my parents aren't going to like this. What about your mom? Did all those years in Europe rub off on her, too, or will she not be as chill with this as you're pretending she will?"

"I don't care what my mother thinks. I love her, but she doesn't — and never has — run my life. And neither should yours."

"Way to avoid answering the question." Swinging my legs toward the side of the bed, I jumped off and swiped my pants up from the floor, hopping into them as he sighed. "I don't know why I thought it was a good idea to even give this a chance, because I know my parents won't understand."

"So, you would rather walk away, instead of believing that perhaps your mom and dad will just be happy for you?"

I finished buttoning my pants, then looked up to frown at him. "God, are you really that naïve? They aren't going to overlook the fact we're cousins, Banner, no matter how much we like each other."

"I more than merely like you, Val. In the morning, you're the first person I think of and the same thing at night while I'm lying in bed. Ever since we walked into each other at the club, I've wanted to do things to you..." He blew out a breath and strode toward me, hands in the pockets of his jeans, as if he didn't trust himself enough to even touch me in this moment. "Fuck, I wait for your first text of the day and count down the hours until we're in the same room, alone. All so I can take advantage of the little time we have together."

His words, mixed with the fire in his eyes, made me gasp as he stopped in front of me, his bare chest brushing lightly against the fabric of my bra. My eyes fluttered closed as his hands found their way to my waist, where he caressed my bare skin with the pads of his thumbs as my arms found their way around his neck of their own accord.

There wasn't any denying how much I wanted him, not when he could touch me, and all thought except to get closer to him fled from my mind.

"Stay with me," he whispered into my ear, grabbing the lobe between his teeth and biting gently before releasing it after a quick suck. "Don't think about it. Just... give me time. Let me show you why we're perfect for each other."

God, I wanted to, more than anything in the world, especially as my body responded to his teasing. My heart beat faster, my thighs squeezed together to try and quell the ache that rose in between them with need. Things wouldn't be as bad as I thought it would be when our family found out, would it? I wanted to think that because walking away would suck, especially this moment.

He breathed in, I breathed out, and all the while we shared every single breath between us.

When he kissed me, for a few brief seconds our hearts beat in unison. Our hands were all over each other, giving into the passion we wanted to explore so desperately. More and more until we were mixed and mingled and tangled up in each other, with neither of us knowing where the other began or ended.

Yet, when he tried to lead me back onto the bed, all I could think about was how my family would react. In my heart, I knew their response wouldn't be good. I grew up with them, understood the way they thought, and this wasn't something they would approve of.

Six days of bliss, but accompanied by the tightness in my chest that wouldn't go away? The one that knew we couldn't do this no matter how right everything felt between us or how much we were both attracted to each other?

So, I broke away with a soft, sorrow-filled cry that only accelerated the hurt in my heart. "No, Banner."

I couldn't stomach the devastation in his eyes as he stepped away from me, the woman he wanted and couldn't have. His expression changed to one of reluctant acceptance the more I spoke.

"We can't do this." The words flew from my mouth as I finished dressing, put on my shoes and grabbed my coat from the nearby chair. "I thought...maybe, for a moment, we could do this. But this is madness. Our family...no matter what we want, we can't do this to them, because if they don't accept it, we're going to rip them apart."

"I get your point of view, Val, but—"

"No." Slipping my arms into my coat, I zipped it up and grabbed my scarf, wrapping it around my neck before crossing my arms over my chest. "Don't, Banner. I love my parents and I know them enough to know this would hurt them. I've been ignoring it, trying to tell myself otherwise, but I can't ignore it any longer. I've got...I've got to stop this before it's too late... before..."

My voice trembled with emotion, leaving me unable to finish the thought.

The one where I might admit to having already began falling for him, to how being with him just felt right from the moment we met... even though it was so, so wrong.

He knew, though. That's when he stepped forward with a soft, "Shh," and wrapped me in his embrace, resting his chin atop my head. We stood that way for a few moments, until I could take a deep breath without it wobbling. That's when he cupped my cheek in his hand, tipping my head back until our eyes met.

"How about one last kiss?" He smirked at my sigh, his thumb caressing my cheek as he winked. "Just one, Val, because you're walking away, and I want to give you something to remember me by."

My consent was granted when I tilted my cheek into his touch, my eyes closing as his face descended toward mine. Our lips met for an agonizing, delicious kiss I wouldn't forget for a long time, if not my entire life. It was bittersweet, powerful, with no inch of our bodies touching except for our lips. There wasn't any doubt in my mind that we wouldn't see much of each other after this. We couldn't, unless we wanted to end up like this once more, wanting and needing yet unable to quench our thirst for each other.

And when the kiss ended, I didn't even look at him. I couldn't.

If I had, me leaving would never happen.

Instead, I forced myself to grab my purse, leave his

room, and make my way out of his apartment without a backward glance.

That moment would become the defining moment of each encounter we had for years after. He wanted, I denied, and our need simmered beneath the surface until neither of us could ignore it any longer.

CHAPTER 8

JUNE 1ST

THE NEXT TIME WE LAID EYES ON EACH OTHER CAME A little shy of two and a half years after I walked out.

I sat on the lap of my boyfriend, the one throwing the party, when I spotted him after he walked in the door.

At first, not being able to see his face, I didn't realize it was him thanks to his short, cropped hair, along with the fact he looked like he'd just come from some rich person's fundraiser in the suit he wore. And, maybe he had, which made me question why a guy like that would come to a party like this.

But then he lifted his gaze and surveyed the crowd of people in a slow, languid manner before sweeping past me. Only for his gorgeous eyes to return seconds later, glinting in the light an instant before his expression hardened. His lips twisted as he recognized me at the same moment I realized who he was.

Although I completely understood his expression of displeasure, a tilt of my head to the side and a lift of my brow made him glare at me harder before turning away.

Fine then, if that's the way he wanted to play it, I could pretend we hadn't seen each other. My current boyfriend made the decision easier by wrapping his arms around my waist from behind to grab my attention.

"Baby…" He purred as one arm across my chest tugged me back toward his, the other slipping down my body toward the space exposed by my short skirt and then between my slightly parted legs. "You're tense. You wanna feel good yeah?"

I did want to feel good — I always had — but he didn't do that for me. Too long since any other man had, although I faked my pleasure quite well. It was hard to maintain a relationship with a man who never failed to notice my lack of orgasm from our encounters and considered getting me off as a challenge.

So, when a man touched me, all I did was close my eyes and think of the one who would always be the one for me in that way. The entire time, he remained in my thoughts, even though he only touched me once in that way. I would think about how his kiss made my heart race and my toes curl, which made me come so hard it was impossible to hold back a scream.

And there he stood across the room, smiling and

laughing and shaking people's hands, not even sneaking slight glances my way.

He pretended we weren't anywhere near each other.

Why would I expect any different? These last couple years, we hadn't spoken. No phone calls, no texts, no visits to my parent's house. Not even for my commencement ceremony, where I graduated summa cum laude, my family cheering for me loudly enough to embarrass me.

I wished to see him there so bad, to hear even a civil 'hello' from his beautiful, deep voice while he undressed me with his eyes.

Instead he froze me out with complete and utter silence, which I completely deserved considering he wasn't the one who walked out. Expecting anything from him, even now when we were at the same party by complete coincidence, would be stupid.

With that in mind, I turned in my boyfriend's arms and slipped my hand down his right one. Interlacing our fingers together, I lead him toward the stairs. He wasn't what I wanted, but in this moment, he would be what I got since I couldn't have the person every single inch of me truly desired.

We didn't even make it into the room once we were up the steps. He pushed me toward the wall outside the bedroom door, lifted my skirt from behind, and ground his arousal against my back. He kissed the nape of my neck while the soft clanking noises gave away the unbuckling of his belt.

I waited for the moment he would shove himself inside of me with no preparation, as he usually did. The pain would make me hiss and take my mind off everything I couldn't have for even a few moments.

Yet the thrust, the pain, it never came, because all I heard was him groaning and then his body disappeared from against mine.

Banner cursed and there were what I could only assume were *his* hands on my skirt, bringing it back down to cover my exposed ass. His free hand grabbed my left upper arm and dragged me into the nearby bedroom. It was dark, my eyes adjusting only seconds before the door shut and the lock clicked, and I was being whirled around as the ceiling light came on.

There he stood, hands on his hips and lips curled in disgust as he spat, "What the fuck are you doing, Val?"

"Me? You're the one who just assaulted my boyfriend!"

If I hadn't seen it myself, I would've never known how much worse a disgusted look could get, but Banner managed it with an even nastier snarl. "That piece of shit was your boyfriend? Wow, Val, do you enjoy shit like that now? Being exposed in front of a bunch of strangers?"

As if I was going to answer that. "Don't act like you care about me all of a sudden."

His expression softened only to tighten again when someone knocked on the door, which made him shout. "Leave her the fuck alone, asshole, unless you want me to kick your goddamn ass!"

When there wasn't any response, he crossed his arms over his chest and shook his head. "What the hell happened to you, Val?"

"Nothing, *Brad*. At least, nothing that's any of your fucking business." I waved my hand at the door to indicate the party downstairs. "This is my going away party and your presence is ruining it. Let me out of this room and get out of here, thank you very much."

He frowned. "Going away party? Where are you going?"

"London!" I spread my arms wide and laughed. "Isn't that some funny ass irony? For a year, I'll be where you used to live, but I'll be working." I stepped forward, until we were inches apart, and stabbed him in the chest, glaring up at his stupid lovely face. "Far, far away from you."

I thought he might snap back at me or say something mean, yet he didn't. All I saw was sadness and worry in his eyes, which I hated because we both knew the only person I had anger at was myself.

And my heart hurt when he merely whispered, "I'll be sad when you're halfway across the world, Val." That's when I knew he had already spent the last two years being sad. His hurt, like mine, wouldn't go away any time soon.

Even though we hadn't dated long, I knew the depth of his feelings at the time were more serious than mine. Me walking away hadn't happened soon enough to avoid the very thing I walked away for. Well, except for our parents, who were never made aware of the brief almost-serious relationship.

But he would have to get over it.

Nothing could happen.

We were never going to have each other in our lives like we wanted and apparently, anything else was too painful.

"You'll be fine," I assured him, going to step around him only to have him grasp my upper arm to stop me from leaving. "What?"

"I'm sorry if you thought I didn't care or never thought about you. That couldn't be further from the truth, Val, and..."

"And what? Anything you say will be empty, meaningless words now, you know that?" I jerked my arm free and strode to the door, begging the tears aching to roll down my cheeks to wait until I was alone to fall. "Go get on with your life and don't try to shove your way into mine, where you're not wanted."

My words were harsh, and I knew it, but what else could I do? I couldn't breathe while in the same room with him, wanting to touch him yet knowing it wasn't a good idea to do so. Every time I had to deny myself, a little part inside died a quiet death of desperation.

"Wait." He came up behind me and put his hands on my waist. My whole body tightened with awareness as he bent his head to whisper in my ear, "One last kiss, Val, before you leave. That's all I want."

"That isn't a good idea."

"Probably not, but one last kiss won't change anything."

Of course not, yet did he care? No. He knew me; understood everything said between us would do nothing more than ensure we didn't start something neither of us were willing to finish. His desire for a kiss wasn't anything more than a little harmless fun.

I remembered the last time we kissed goodbye and how he haunted my dreams for a long time after that. However, I didn't remember how it felt in his embrace, with his lips on mine. And here was the opportunity to refresh my memory, to take something of him along for the trip.

So, turning in his arms, I allowed him to press me back against the door with his strong, lithe form and put his mouth on mine, where he teased his way in by running his tongue along my lips. This time, though, when he tangled his tongue with mine, everything had changed between us and he wasn't as gentle.

His disappointment, worry, and sadness came through in a kiss meant to steal my breath, a feat he managed as his hands grabbed my waist and he ground against me like my boyfriend tried to a little while ago. Only this time, my body responded with an urgency for more. I clenched my thighs together, seeking to push the reaction away before I did something stupid like give into everything I'd spent the last couple years running from.

And with that thought, I tore my lips from his and pushed at his shoulders. "There, you got what you wanted. Now back the fuck up so I can get out of here."

Reluctance clear, he nodded, then kissed my forehead before dropping his hands away. "Have a good trip, Val. Try to get out and enjoy London while you're there, all right?"

"Yeah, I will."

I meant the words when I said them, but by the time I got home and into my room, the tears ran free. My heart and body wanted the one man it shouldn't want, let alone ever have.

Suddenly, no number of miles seemed far enough to ease the ache in my heart or the desire refusing to go away no matter who I dated or slept with. His touch had awakened something in me that nobody else ever had or might ever again.

But then, I dried my tears, because I knew better than anyone else that nothing lasts forever. That meant one day he wouldn't have this sort of power over me or my body any longer.

Too bad lying to myself only lasted for so long before reality slapped me in the face.

"THIS IS FOR YOU, HONEY." MY MOTHER HANDED ME an envelope, unable to hide her curiosity. "Doesn't have anything except your name on it. Who's it from?"

One sight at my name written in cursive and I knew exactly who it was from.

"Uh, it's from Banner."

I recognized his handwriting from all the times I sat on his lap while he worked, waiting while he wrote down information and signed things.

"Oh." She sat at the table and quirked a brow. "I didn't know you two were so close."

"We're not." Only my mother would think an envelope with only my name on it meant something significant. "I ran into him at the party the other night. No idea what's in this."

She said nothing, so I ripped it open and peeked inside, only to find a surprising and sizable stack of £100 notes wrapped up in a short note that read:

Val, for your trip. If you need anything while you're there, call the number listed below and mention my name. Trust me. Any time, any place, don't be afraid to reach out. I'll miss you. ~Banner

My mother's eyes widened at the stack of money sitting in front of me and laughed. "What in the world? Did you ask him for help?"

"No, Mom. You know me better than that."

"Of course, I do. I'm surprised is all. Did you two discuss your internship?"

"I told him I was working there, which is the truth. I didn't mention the fact it's unpaid except for housing and meals. This was nice of him, but..." I picked up the envelope and shoved the money back inside. "I'll return it to him before heading to the airport."

"Sweetie..."

I shook my head, cutting her off and then smiled. "I've got enough from my job here that I saved. I don't need his money, or want it, for that matter."

She sighed, reached across the table, and covered my hand with hers. "All right, dear. Tell him I said hello, won't you? I'm terribly sad I won't be able to take you to the airport tomorrow."

"Thanks, Mom. Me, too, but it isn't far, and I've got to be there so early. It would be boring for anyone who tagged along, especially after they tightened security."

"You're right." With that, she pushed back her chair and stood up, yawning. "I'll see you in the morning, sweetheart."

"Night, Mom."

She exited the kitchen after blowing a kiss, leaving me

alone at the table with my thoughts, ones she would never be privy to. A part of me wanted to stalk over to Banner's place to give him a piece of my mind.

However, I didn't. And on the way to the airport the next morning, I didn't stop at his place either. Instead, I kept the money tucked inside the envelope and zipped up in my bag, where it would stay until my return a year later.

To me, the money represented more than the mere kindness of a cousin. It was help from a man who wanted to take care of me, who didn't seem to have the power like I did to walk away from a situation that wouldn't lead anywhere good.

Until I came back home, my plan remained to not acknowledge him in any way, shape, or form.

If only the universe would cooperate before I did something stupid.

And following nine months of blissful peace in London, I headed to Paris for two weeks... which is when our worlds collided in a way that truly would change everything forever.

CHAPTER 9
MARCH 15TH

"VAL?"

Surely, my ears weren't hearing the last man I wanted to see with my name on his lips? The one who couldn't possibly be in the same place and time as me when we'd had zero contact.

Then again, I'd been drinking for three hours at a local pub and now stood against the wall just to the left of where my new friends sat at, a little bit unsteady on my feet.

Maybe if I ignored him, pretended he wasn't there, then he would go away without saying another word to me.

Fat chance since he stepped closer, his familiar scent and heat approaching me until he leaned back beside me and bent a little to whisper in my ear. "I won't let you act like you don't see me. I'll stand here until you agree to talk to me."

No doubt. "In that case, I'll leave."

I pushed away from the wall, but he put an arm around my waist and stepped closer, until his body covered half of mine.

"Please, Val," he begged, the words barely audible above the loud music even though he said them close to my ear. "Let's go somewhere private and chat."

As if that's all he wanted. I could feel the heat emanating off his body. Even now, my own responded with all the suppressed emotions of the last few years. I wanted nothing more than to give into the banked passion between us.

"We can't."

This time he whispered his answer directly into my ear. The arm around my waist tightened for a moment before slipping down the other side and interlacing our fingers together. "Yes, we can, Val, and we will, because out of all the places in the world I could walk into... we're both in this one, just like that night at the party? This is more than coincidence, Val. I'm tired of denying myself the one thing I want more than anything else in this entire fucking world."

God, me too. More than I'd ever admit out loud to him or anyone else.

I melted into his arms when his mouth moved from my ear to my neck, his teeth sliding across the sensitive skin there until the only sound I could manage to make was a soft, longing sigh of capitulation.

At some point, I must've said okay or given him a positive response because he dragged me out of the club after grabbing my coat. Before I knew what was happening or could even say goodbye to my friends, we were in the back of a taxi. His hand grasped mine firmly, as if he were afraid I would disappear at any second.

I would have fled if it weren't for the need coursing through me the same way his own shined from his eyes.

Doing what we wanted would be reckless and unforgivable if our families found out. But we were thousands of miles away and there wasn't any reason to deny ourselves here.

That's how I convinced myself to go through with it; to follow him out of the taxi and into the hotel where he must've been staying, then up the elevator to his room. He behaved the entire way up, neither of us touching each other except for our connected hands. Not once did I glance his way even though I felt his gaze burning a hole into the side of my head.

I didn't know why I did it. Maybe I was trying to hurt him, to keep him wondering if I would really go through with it, or I didn't trust what he might see in my eyes. I had never been good at hiding how I felt and I didn't want him to realize the true depth of my feelings for him.

Or perhaps it was because no matter what happened tonight, a long-term relationship between us — something serious leading to a lifetime together — would never happen. Why bother putting a stop to the inevitable next step of our mutual attraction when we both knew it would lead nowhere anyway?

Tonight, I would give into him and we would hopefully get our fill of each other, enough to never dare do something like this again.

That's why I let him lead me to the hotel room, open the door, and shut us inside in the room. The moonlight shone through the huge windows, illuminating the space enough we could almost see each other clearly. I let him slide my coat off my shoulders, where it slipped to the floor, and my dress soon followed, baring me to his hungry gaze, as the only thing left covering me were a pair of nude silk panties.

All of which didn't prevent me from smirking and commenting, "I thought you said you wanted to talk."

"We will. Later."

I understood. In reality, the last thing I wanted to do was talk, especially since we were both on fire, aching to be skin-to-skin with each other.

He stepped forward and swept me up into his arms. Stalking toward the bed, he laid me upon it gently as if I were something infinitely precious.

I didn't argue. There wasn't a point, after all, considering we were only minutes away from giving into something that had built between us for years. He stood beside the bed, removing his clothing fast and furiously, almost as if they burned him.

And maybe they did since I felt on fire too, like if he didn't touch me, I would burst into flames.

When he finished, he climbed onto the bed and hovered over my body. His lips brushed against mine before he asked in a hushed voice, "Is this okay, Val? As much as I want you, what happens next is up to you."

"Oh, please, Banner. We're in your hotel room despite me walking away. Don't tell me it's up to me, not now."

He stared down at me. A multitude of emotions I couldn't discern flashed across his face before disappearing, leaving only passionate need in its wake. He said nothing, tension growing between us until he finally decided. Groaning, he captured my mouth with his, demanding entrance by running his tongue along my lips.

I caved, sliding my arms around his neck and lifting my hips, reciprocating with a moan of my own because my entire body felt alive, electrified. My scalp tingled as he shoved his fingers into my hair, angling my head in just a way he could kiss me deeper and harder, his body finally pressing mine into the mattress with its delicious weight.

In that moment, nothing would've stopped us from having sex. The entire world could have shaken or burned up and I wouldn't have let go of him, wouldn't have wanted to do anything except feel him on top of me, or dare to miss the proof of how much he wanted me. We were both crazy with denied desire, but finally giving in left me wondering if I had a mistake all those years ago, because there wasn't any denying how amazing it felt to finally experience his bare body against mine.

I hated myself a little, especially as he dragged his mouth away to kiss down my body, stopping at my breasts to lick and kiss them, my hands now tangled in his hair. Eventually, as I continued to move my hips, desperate for his touch there, he moved further down and removed the soft fabric in one smooth motion down my legs.

Then, he took his hands and spread them wide, his breath hot as his mouth made contact, making me gasp and tug a little on his hair. Little noises escaped from me as he nipped, licked, and sucked. His fingers joined in until my orgasm took over and his self-satisfied chuckle irritated me a tiny bit as my whole body shook.

Not that my exasperation lasted long as he slid back up my body, giving me a taste of myself when he kissed me again while using one hand to guide his cock's entry inside me.

And fuck, I hated both of us right then. I hated the way this felt so wrong and yet so right, as we fit perfectly together. Every slide in and out we gasped, moaned and sighed in unison, which only made things worse, because it made me question everything I'd always known as true.

How could sex with Banner be so fucking amazing when all my previous attempts with other men never reached this level of terrific? How could he get me off with his mouth and hands, yet I never experienced much of a tingle of arousal by anyone else?

All I could think is that it was mental. That somewhere in my mind refused to accept anyone else because a part of me always wanted him no matter how terrible of an idea I thought it would be.

That had to be it because I came a second time, he followed quickly after, and never, ever since being with someone had I ever had such a level of comfort lying in someone's arms following sex with them as I had lying in bed with Banner after.

So, tears rolled down my cheeks, and when he wrapped me in his arms, I only cried harder since there wasn't anything else to do except go with it. To release all those long-held back feelings and emotions for this entire situation...for him.

Later, after I stopped crying, he tried to talk to me finally, but it was too late. It wasn't right how... well, right how everything felt with Banner, and tonight didn't change anything no matter how much he must have hoped it would.

Okay, and me. A tiny bit of me that would love to ignore the reality of our relationship wouldn't be convinced over the rest of my rational mind. Plus my heart knew doing anything together beyond tonight wasn't anything more than a pipe dream.

That's why I distracted him with a kiss so he wouldn't continue trying to get me to talk to him, which led to another round of sex, and we fell asleep afterward.

Then, a little before the sun came up, I sneaked out of his bed, and got dressed. Fishing the money he had left in my mailbox what felt like a lifetime ago out of my purse, I put it on the kitchen counter along with a little note asking him to please leave me alone now. To stop chasing me because no matter what our hearts wanted, we were never, ever going to be together like he wanted.

After, I left the hotel room as quietly as I could manage without waking him up, and didn't look back, despite how many tears fell free as I did so.

It would have been the perfect way to end things if things were fair and the world didn't find playing games so amusing.

Because, of course, that wasn't the end of us, at all, but merely the beginning of an entirely different degree of fucked up.

CHAPTER 10
JUNE 16TH

GOD, I THOUGHT THINGS COULDN'T GET WORSE, BUT I wanted nothing more than to go back to the night with Banner and slap some sense into myself.

Why?

Why?

Because I ignored the signs even knowing we hadn't used protection that night, like fucking idiots.

So, for two months, I deliberately ~~pushed~~ assigned the fact my period hadn't arrived and that I felt like barfing every day, all day the entire time.

For a month more, I refused to acknowledge the positive sign on the goddamn pregnancy test. Well, other than to pick up prenatal vitamins and hide them somewhere so nobody would know my secret.

And as I finally headed home upon the end of my internship, I pretended there hadn't been a need to go out and use what little remained of my savings to buy a pair of maternity pants just so I could wear fucking pants that buttoned.

There wouldn't be much room for denial once I landed in Cleveland because I would have to make a decision about what to do.

At thirteen weeks, I didn't have an infinite amount of time to figure out where to go from here. I examined all the options — abortion, adoption, or keeping the baby — and none of them seemed like a good idea full out.

I wasn't for or against abortion in general. In fact, I never thought about it until I found myself in this situation. All I knew was, having a baby had always been in my future life. Something that would happen, just not now. And especially not with my damn cousin, of all the potential partners in the world.

Yet, I didn't know if I could live with myself if I chose that option and that's why I hadn't. Any doubt at all meant it wouldn't be a good idea to go through with something so permanent.

Then, there was adoption. Question was, could I live knowing there was a child out there that was half mine and half his? And never knowing a thing about that child unless they decided they wanted to find me when they were grown? Could I live with that? With what could be in the future, knowing I might have to explain to my future partner about the child and how all that came around?

No. No, I didn't think I could and that's why I sat on the flight home, crying my eyes out much to the consternation and concern of the woman sitting next to me. Because the only option left had me showing up to Banner's work or apartment, three months after we had sex to tell him our entire lives were about to change forever.

How would I face my parents? His mother?

What were they going to say when they found out what we had done?

All the effort I put into not hurting them, not doing something I knew they wouldn't understand... and I fucked it up with one stupid, idiotic night where I gave into my heart instead of listening to my head.

Stupid.

I'd been stupid.

And in six months, Banner and I were going to have a baby.

Shit.

***

MY MOTHER, THRILLED TO SEE ME AFTER A YEAR away, hugged me the moment the front door shut, tears springing to each of our eyes.

No point in trying to avoid her embrace. When she pulled away, I grabbed the lapels of my jacket to keep it shut, hoping she wouldn't notice the already tiny little curve of my stomach.

She didn't seem to, although she stepped back and raised her brows, laughing. "Have you put on a little weight, honey?"

"Uh, yeah." I didn't think the fifteen pounds I gained these last two months were noticeable, but apparently I was wrong. "The food in London was delicious and completely irresistible."

Glad that made complete sense as she nodded and I sighed with relief. It wasn't that I wouldn't tell her, I just didn't plan to say anything until I had to. Well, okay, and once I told Banner first because he should know before anybody else.

"How long do you think you'll be staying here, sweetheart?"

"Um, I don't know."

And I didn't. Could be as little as a few weeks once both she and my father knew about my pregnancy, especially since I didn't have a job or even any interviews in the works. It had taken all my energy to make it through this last month of my internship with how nauseous I was all the time, so I hadn't taken the time to apply for anything before coming home.

"Well, that's all right." She turned away and headed toward the living room as I trailed behind her. "You can take as long as you need. You know your dad and I love having you here with us."

"I know. Thanks, Mom."

She smiled over her shoulder as we passed the stairs, taking the left down the hall as I headed toward my room with my luggage.

One look at the warm, cozy, and familiar bed just waiting for me to climb inside was all the convincing I needed to decide the talk with Banner could wait until tomorrow. Today, I was exhausted from everything including the flight and sleep was the most important item on my immediate agenda.

It wasn't long before my comforter covered every inch of my body and I slept soundly through the night, not even a hint of a dream disturbing my much-needed rest.

THE CASINO LOOKED THE SAME, ALTHOUGH THE DUDE checking IDs at the front door the next day had changed, and he seemed to disbelieve my ID for a few seconds before letting me inside. Not before he checked me out with a quick flash of his eyes from my head to my toes and back again, though.

A few months ago, I might've found this flattering, because he wasn't bad looking and had a nice smile. Now, however, it merely bothered me, like some evolutionary part of me understood he wasn't the father of the child I carried and refused to entertain the notion of someone else finding me attractive.

I wasn't sure I'd find Banner here tonight. I thought about calling him, except I couldn't. Why? Because I had deleted his number to keep myself from doing exactly that in my weak moments when I wanted to hear his voice. Chances were he would be working instead of at home, so here I stood in the lobby, trying to will my feet to walk toward the elevator that led to his office.

Everything looked different, although nothing in the casino had changed since I had last stepped inside.

That was the thing though, wasn't it? The way everything looked, felt, seemed... it was all me. I had been the one to leave, to become different, and now this place along with many others would never appear the same as they had in the past.

Yet, unlike a lot of other places, such as home, there was a feeling of warmness in my chest as I stood there, unable to get the picture of me and Banner inside the room not far from me. I could still feel his fingers on my body, his mouth on mine, and part of me ached to turn around, to run as far away as I fucking could.

From him, from the way he made me feel, from everything. But, I couldn't, because we were going to have a child together, and yes, we would need to co-parent because I didn't want to do this on my own.

I didn't know how I would explain things to my own family yet. Every time my parents were around, I thought about how I would tell them what happened as we sat around the dining table, or in the living room. Each scenario ended up with them disappointed and disgusted, while I cried from having been the one to let them down.

Dammit, I should've kept saying no. No to him, no matter the country we were in or how many times we ran into each other at the weirdest times. A thousand times no and I wouldn't be in this position, wondering how the hell I was going to get on that elevator to break the news.

"Are you all right?"

The sound of a man's voice snapped me out of my daze. My face flushed with embarrassment at discovering the man talking to me was none other than Banner's partner, Sam.

He smirked when I took a step back, grabbed my arm as I wobbled, and softly said, "Whoa, there. Do you need to have a seat?"

"Um, no, thank you."

When I pulled my arm back, he let go with a shrug, and gave a quick glance back over his shoulder before smiling at me again. "Heard you went to London. How'd you find it?"

"It was okay, I guess."

He nodded and continued to stare at me, which is when I knew Banner told him what happened... especially when his smile turned into a grin as he asked, "You're here to see Brad, yeah?"

"You know I am."

"Last I heard, you told him never to speak to you again. Changed your mind, have you?"

"Um..." I answered him even though this really wasn't any of his damn business, but maybe he would know where Banner was. "I need to talk to him about something."

That's when I made unmistakable motion. Grabbing the edges of my jacket, I pulled it tighter around my body, and it was like I drew his eyes right to my stomach. In reality, he probably couldn't tell from that alone, but that mixed with my words must've clued him in because his eyes rounded as they found mine again.

Yet, he didn't say a word about it. If anything, he looked worried and the new smile on his face was totally fake as he said, "I'm headed to lunch. Join me."

"I don't—"

He cut me off. "You must be hungry." Grabbing my elbow, he leaned in and whispered, "Trust me, sweetheart. Come with me."

Fuck, suddenly he had me worried, even though his hold was gentle and his words even softer. I didn't know where we were going — okay, I barely knew this fucking man either — yet I let him lead me toward the restaurant until we sat in a booth in the back, well hidden from view.

That's when he finally acknowledged what we both knew with a pointed lift of one brow. "Three months?"

"Yes." He said nothing in reply and after a nervous sip of water, I hoped to change the subject by asking, "Were you in London, too?"

"I usually am. Brad typically takes care of things here." His laughter was more self-deprecating than amused as he added, "I supply the money."

"Oh. I didn't know that."

"Of course not. Most people don't."

The waiter arrived then and we ordered drinks, which were delivered not even a minute later. That's when Sam got straight to the point.

"You two haven't spoken."

"Nope. I was trying not to ever speak to him again."

"As we've established." He took a sip of his drink and shook his head. "This isn't news he's prepared to hear."

"Nor was I."

"Why the wait, darling?"

"I couldn't believe it." I took another few drinks, unsure why I was telling Sam, yet figuring maybe it would be easier to tell Banner next. "I was... well, in denial."

"That is clear." He sighed as I looked down and reached across the table, his voice filled with understanding. "There is no reason to feel ashamed as you do, love."

I laughed at that. "You're kidding right? You do understand the situation, don't you?"

"I do, love."

Something told me he knew all about it, so I focused on his use of a pet name on me. "Why are you calling me darling and love?"

"Habit. It's an English thing." His smile went a bit sheepish then and that's when he looked over my shoulder before the smile turned a bit sad. "There's something you should know."

The weight of his words hit me, my stomach sinking to the floor because I knew something wasn't good when he pulled me along to this corner. The desire to get sick returned. "What?"

"You've arrived just in time for the party."

Confused, that's when I finally looked around and noticed my surroundings. All of them.

The decorated tables rearranged to leave a gigantic circle in the middle of the room.

The hanging blue and silver streamers.

And the sign hanging on the wall that said, *Congratulations, Brad and Sylvia!*

Even though I had no idea what they were being congratulated on, the color drained from my face as sympathy took over Sam's entire expression. Tears began streaming down my cheeks.

Fuck, there wasn't any way I could sit here for a moment longer.

With a desperate stumble from the booth, my eyes pleaded with Sam to get me the hell out of here before I ran into him, before I had to explain my presence to him and whoever this Sylvia was. But the rapid change in Sam's expression to one of false cheerfulness told me it was too late to run now.

Banner spoke from behind me, his voice filled with bewilderment. "Val?"

Unable to turn and face him, I did what I thought any girl in my predicament would do.

I hyperventilated, jerked my begging and tearful gaze up to meet Sam's eyes, and fainted right there on the spot.

CHAPTER 11

JUNE 17TH

"That was quite a tumble." Sam's words had a layer of amusement beneath them as I woke up on an unfamiliar bed, in a rather dark room, and sat up with a gasp. "No need to cause yourself a panic. You're in one of the adjoining hotel suites and there is nobody here except you and I."

Remembering what happened, I snatched up a pillow and smacked him with it hard, snarling at him as he stood up from his perch on my side of the bed. "You're a fucking asshole."

"What?"

"You led me right into the party where there wouldn't be any avoiding him!"

"That wasn't my intention, love. Let—"

"Stop calling me that, dammit." I tossed another pillow at him, throwing the blankets aside and standing up, only to gasp as my head spun. "Fuck, what the hell is wrong with me?"

Sam seemed to have all the answers as he pointed at the tray sitting on a nearby table. "I've taken the liberty of ordering you some dinner. You need to eat."

"Oh, did you? How kind." It was, truly, but my comment was more snide than anything and I searched the room, looking for my shoes. "I need to go home."

"He's waiting outside, love."

Obvious he wouldn't quit with the pet names, I ground my teeth and stalked across the room, finally locating my shoes. Dropping into the chair, I slid into them, only for my stomach to growl at the whiff of whatever deliciousness awaited me under the dish cover. Then, I realized what he said and dropped my head into my hands with a shaky, "Why?"

His words were more hushed as he approached, sitting in the chair opposite me as he continued. "He wants to know why you're here and what you wanted. I've told him he would need to speak with you about that."

"Oh, god, Sam." Jerking my head up, I shook it. "I can't tell him. Not now. He's engaged, isn't he?"

"Yes."

"But... so quick? I mean, only three months have passed!"

"They were mates in school." His sad smile arrived

again as he sat forward and brushed a lock of hair away from my face. "They met up in Paris shortly after..."

He didn't state the obvious and I didn't need him to.

Of course, what he said made sense. I left Banner and told him to leave me alone and that's exactly what he had done. No texts, no calls, nothing.

Then, he turned around, ran into an old friend in Paris, and struck up a romance... "But, so soon?"

Sam laughed. "Her idea, I think. She's ready to have a family and he adores her, I'm afraid. Always has. I believe he would give her anything she wished for."

"Yeah." I agreed even as my own chest burned with heat. Nothing more than mere jealousy at this Sylvia having the one man I couldn't have and never should've touched. "He's a good man that way."

What the hell would I do now?

A few beats of silence Sam scooted his chair closer and held my hands, his whole demeanor intense as he stared at me. "We met in London when you returned a week later and met for a drink."

"What—?"

He continued, giving my hands a bit of a squeeze while shaking his head. "I was there briefly, that's the truth. That's when we slept together. We've been together ever since but been so wound up in each other I haven't mentioned the fact we spent time with one another."

Was he saying...? No way. "Sam, that's nice, but this isn't a game."

"No game, love. I wouldn't play with your emotions that way, not in your state."

"Oh, my god." I pulled my hands from his grip and blew out a harsh breath. "You want to pretend we're a couple, that we've been hiding that fact from Banner, and claim the baby as your own? Do you realize how fucked up that is?"

"I do." His hands moved to my knees, his entire expression earnest and sincere. "I saw the look in your eyes. You don't want to tell him. Hell, you don't wish to tell your family because you're a crazy American—" He laughed when I glared at him and then winked at me. "A woman from a country filled with people who think sleeping with your first cousin is disgusting. Well, love, we don't have that problem in my country."

"Hardly an issue considering you're not my cousin, Sam." When he merely grinned, I sighed, frustrated. "I mean, why in the hell would you want to do this and potentially alienate your business partner?"

"I wouldn't worry about that, darling."

"Stop calling me that. Do you even know my name?"

He stuck out a hand, grabbing mine and shaking it, eyes dancing with humor. "Valerie, it's a pleasure to make your acquaintance once more. The name's Samwell but you may call me Sam."

"Or crazy, because you're the crazy one here, Sam. Stop fucking around and tell me what to do."

"I am." He didn't miss a beat or even so much as blink. "Marry me."

My heart pounded. "What? Sam—"

"You'll never want for money, Val. We could live here or in England. I would love to show you my home. You don't ever have to see him again if you don't want. He'll never know."

"Oh please, Sam." My nose tingled and a single tear slipped down my cheek because I hadn't expected this when I left the house today. "You don't know me, at all. Why are you doing this? Tell me why."

"Because he is my best friend, love. And we're both smart enough to know he'll drop Sylvia in a heartbeat if he finds out you're having his child. He and I, we've been mates since the day he started school after moving to England and I would do anything to spare him pain. It hasn't worked between you two and a child won't change that."

I understood. I never wanted to hurt Banner. In the moment, what Sam said made sense, even though it wasn't clear why he threw himself straight into the fire.

"You don't need to marry me to avoid hurting him, Sam. Don't you think he'll get pissed when he finds out what you want to pretend we've been hiding?"

"I've had a bit of a thing for you, love, since the first

time I saw you inside the casino. I just never said anything."

What he for real? Hard to tell. "Sure you did."

He smirked. "Trust me. He'll be fine."

"Oh, like I did earlier?"

He chuckled and leaned in, pressing a chaste kiss to my lips before I knew what his intentions were. "As my wife, you'll need to trust me."

I lifted a hand to my lips, pressing against where his lips met mine in an attempt to figure out how I felt about that little action. At the same time, there was a loud knock at the door. Then, Banner's voice called out, "Sam. Is she awake yet? Let me the fuck in."

"Well, love." Sam quirked a brow and cocked his head toward the door, his eyes remaining locked on me. "Are you in or out?"

My heart raced, indecisive and thrilled, all at once. What he wanted to do was wrong, I knew that inside and out. But his way would be the one to get me out of this predicament I never thought to find myself in. I didn't know Sam, except from the stuff Banner had shared about him and there hadn't been anything to worry myself over.

Sam did come from money. He had so much money, he never had to work another day in this life, or the next one, if such a thing were true. I didn't believe he would make a proposal like this without being serious and I really didn't want to hurt my family. Or Banner.

Well, I didn't want to hurt anyone, including myself, and there wasn't any way I could face my family to tell them the truth. Nor could I stand the thought of telling my parents I was pregnant and the father wasn't going to be involved, leaving me to raise a child alone.

Yes, I was a coward, I wouldn't deny that.

So, I chose to take the easy way out.

In my head, I told myself... if Banner asked me for the truth, I would have to tell him because I didn't believe I could lie when straight up asked for the truth. I had never been good at it and hoped he wouldn't think anything of it.

Out loud, I smiled at Sam, nodded. "Just one condition."

"Name it, love."

As Banner knocked at the door again, we both stood, with Sam taking my left hand in his as I told him, "You'll have to marry me before the baby comes. My parents will insist upon it."

He lifted my hand to his mouth, kissed the back of it, and grinned. "You got it, darling."

Then, he led me toward the door and swung it open, revealing Banner's worried countenance as he stood there leaning back against the wall.

"Hey, mate," Sam led without hesitation. "She's fine."

A moment, a small glance, that was all it took.

Banner saw our hands intertwined and his look went

from one of caring to one of patent disbelief as he straightened, snarling, "What the hell, man?"

Sam told him the same story he told me inside the room. Banner glanced at me every so often with mixed expressions I couldn't read, although by the end he blurted, "That's a bunch of bullshit. Tell me this isn't true, Val."

"I..." Taking a deep breath, I focused hard on not stuttering, keeping in mind the fact he had gotten engaged to someone else and needed to go be with her. "We're together, Banner. It's true."

And it was, even if that only happened a few minutes ago.

"And getting married?"

"Yes." Glancing down, I steeled myself to tell him the rest, the real reason things were going down this way. I almost couldn't do it when I saw the little bit of pain in his eyes that he tried hard to hide. But, we weren't good for each other and it would never work out, I knew that. So, I put on a bright smile and said, "Plus, I'm pregnant."

That's when Banner cracked.

He punched Sam square in the face before either of us had a chance to step out of the way.

Then, he stormed off without another glance in my direction while I tended to Sam, who held his hand over his nose, laughing like it didn't matter.

Leaving me believing there probably wasn't a chance in hell Banner would ever forgive us for this.

"WHAT DID YOU SAY?" MY MOTHER STARED AT ME, mouth agape, as I sat next to Sam, my hand clenched in his. I was glad for the support as her voice raised a slight bit in disbelief. "You're pregnant?"

"And getting married, Mom," I clarified for the third time. "To Sam."

"But, we don't know him." She dabbed at her wet eyes with a handkerchief while my father sat beside her with a disgruntled yet strangely pleasant expression on his face. "How can you be having a child with someone we've never met until now?"

"I'm sorry." Strange to apologize for something I hadn't ever thought would happen at any point in my life. "I've been so busy, Mom. And, you know, it just... happened."

She sniffled. "Three months?"

"Almost four now." My mother always wanted

grandchildren and no doubt thought my brothers would be the first. Neither of them nor their wives seemed interested having children any time soon though. "I know you're surprised, but so was I. Honestly. You know I wanted to do quite a few things before settling down."

Boy, I had turned into quite the liar.

I wasn't happy with that, at all, yet that actual truth seemed to please her, as she moved her focus from me to Sam, and smiled at him. "You said you're a friend of Banner's?"

"Yes." Sam lifted my hand and kissed the back of it, which I noticed made my mother practically preen with delight, especially when he added, "He introduced us, actually."

"Love at first sight." My mother sighed, as her story about my father talked about how it was that way for them. I never quite believed anything was that simple when it came to relationships. "I bet Banner is happy for you."

"He is."

Oh, I wondered if Sam were too good a liar, too. The mistruths seemed delivered from his tongue with little difficulty, as if he had been practicing for something like this all his life. He embellished and exaggerated the story he made up in that hotel room. It had evolved into this entire romantic wooing I could only wish to have experienced.

Well, all right. Sam treated me like I was precious.

For the last two weeks, since that afternoon in the hotel, Sam visited often. He would come over to join me for breakfast, take me out to lunch, and occasionally charm me with dinner. We would go to the park, the bookstore, the mall; anywhere and everywhere.

And the entire time, I wondered how long it would be until this wasn't something he wanted to do anymore. He wanted me to trust him, yet how could I when our entire relationship had us involved in an elaborate lie? Bigger ones by the day, as well.

Hypocritical of me since it was my fault we were living a lie at all. Part of me wanted to tell him to actually woo me as if he were interested in me and trying to make me fall in love with him. Then I realized, that's exactly what he had been doing.

He did his best to keep my mind off Banner and everything else because we were getting married to each other. I would be having a baby he would be taking responsibility for.

Often, since the entire thing went down, I've thought about what might happen if the child looked like Banner. Would he notice if and when we were ever around him once more?

Then again, I didn't know if that mattered. Banner and I were family. So even if the child did resemble him in quite a few ways, there would be no certainty about whether the child was his, or from us being part of the same family.

Stupid to worry about it, I guessed, since Sam stated his wish was to live in England. Plus living far away from Banner meant less chance he would find out the truth, as well as the more I could work on truly getting over him once and for all.

"Are you okay, love?"

Sam's question jerked me out of my thoughts, where I found my parents and him all staring at me with intense concern. "Oh, sorry. Yeah, I'm fine. Just thinking."

"We'll have so much fun planning your wedding, sweetheart." My mom clapped, her first joyous reaction since our arrival, and rose to her feet. "How long do we have to plan?"

I swallowed, hard, as Sam answered with a cheery, "Val would like to have her wedding before she's showing too much, ma'am. We figured one month for something small and intimate. Family and close friends only."

He meant my family. He told me his family would celebrate on their own once we were across the ocean. Frankly, I was glad for him making that decision, as I wasn't quite sure I could face his family and mine at the same time without cracking.

"We better get to work then, honey."

She hugged me when I got to my feet and understood when I told her it would be better to start tomorrow when I wasn't feeling so worn out. Then she told my father she was going to rest and left the room.

He pulled me into a tight bear hug when she was gone, whispering, "Congratulations," and told Sam he better take good care of his little girl.

A part of me trembled on the inside, relieved they took the news so well, yet saddened at having lied to my parents. How different it would've been with Banner, I had no idea, and perhaps that would be a good thing in hindsight.

Hard to get myself to believe that though.

And as we got into the car for Sam to take me to his place, a tiny little part of me couldn't stop the little seed of doubt in my mind. Was I about to make the biggest mistake of my life or not?

August 2nd

IT TOOK SAM LONGER THAN I LIKED TO PASSIONATELY kiss me.

The first time was at our wedding after the justice of the peace pronounced us husband and wife. Up until that point, nothing more than chaste kisses would pass from his lips to mine and although I noticed, I guess I didn't care to ask why not.

We held hands regularly, but no kissing, and no sex. I wouldn't lie and say I didn't miss sex; after all, I enjoyed it immensely when it felt wonderful. And I did wonder about what sex with him would be like. A lot.

Sam was dashing in his own way. His accent leant a lot in that aspect; it wasn't his entire appeal, however. He wore his dark blond hair slicked back — in the sexy, shiny way, not the sleazy one. His eyes were dark too, almost black in their intensity. In a suit, he was delicious; in jeans and a button-down shirt, he embodied masculinity.

I found him pleasing and it bothered me I had no idea if he would turn me on sexually, especially with all my disappointing encounters in the past. Looking at someone never did that for me; I needed touched and held and kissed to have such knowledge.

And he managed to keep me from completely finding out until our wedding night.

The wedding took place in my parent's backyard, which they had cleaned up and decorated the day before. The entire setup was something close to right out of a fairy-tale. My mother worked hard, which left me convinced I made the right decision. Even though the butterflies in my stomach wouldn't go away when I thought about how I would be someone's wife soon, as well as a mother.

Up until the time to walk down the aisle, I sat in my bedroom, wearing my beautiful dress and veil. My hand was on my slightly rounded stomach as I promised my unborn child I would try to be the best mother possible.

When my father came to get me, I pasted a smile on my face and kept it there. Then, I barely managed to not stumble when I saw Banner sitting among the guests as I walked down the aisle, his new fiancée beside him.

Sam must've invited him.

Not that it mattered, as his eyes burned into mine when we caught each other's gaze for a mere second. They flicked down to my stomach, his lips twisted and he looked away, leaving me breathless and sad.

I knew his eyes remained on me the rest of the time as I stood at the altar. I promised my future to his best friend while everyone watched my lie with happy smiles.

And when Sam lifted my veil to give me our first kiss, his eyes were filled with a fire I never saw from him until that moment. He cupped my face in his hands, leaned in, and whispered against my lips, "Forget about him, love. You're mine now."

Then, he pressed his mouth against mine in a chaste kiss, almost disappointing all my hopes until I felt his tongue seeking entry into my mouth. I let him and it was a lovely, sweet kiss that curled my toes and did allow me to forget about Banner for a few moments.

Our kiss convinced me we would be all right.

He did turn me on, which was a feat all on its own. If his kiss could make my body respond like now, I looked forward to finding out what sex with him would be like when we were alone later.

However, all the hope in the world for my marriage to Sam didn't put Banner far from my mind especially when they remained business partners.

And later, a little incident before we left that evening shook me to the core.

I FINISHED CHANGING OUT OF MY DRESS INTO SOME jeans and a t-shirt seconds before there was a knock at my bedroom door. Figuring it was Sam, I didn't bother to ask before flinging it open, only for Banner to barge past me.

My heart pounded even as I shut the door and turned around to face him, no idea what to say. After a few moments where we stood staring at one another saying nothing, I lifted my chin in defiance as my body quivered with anticipation. "What do you want?"

He smiled, but his eyes weren't happy. They gleamed with an emotion I didn't dare examine as he replied with a simple, "You."

"Banner." I laughed, incredulous, and pointed out the window. "Did you not just see me marry Sam?"

"I did."

"And?"

"And what?" He stalked over until our faces were inches apart and I could feel the heat emanating off him. "Leave you alone, Val? How the hell can I do that when you went and married my fucking business partner and best friend?"

"You do it because you have to, Banner." I hissed the words at him, stabbing him in the chest with one finger as my own anger rose. "You do it because you're engaged to Sylvia."

He chuckled at that. "Tell me the truth, Val."

"About what?"

"Everything. Why you left that morning. Why you showed up at that damn party." Lifting a hand to my face, he pushed a lock of hair behind my ear, his voice softening as he blew me away with his next words. "Why you decided to marry him when you're carrying *my* fucking child."

"W—what?" I managed to gasp out, trying to step back, but he held me closer to him with one arm tight around my waist. "Banner, I..."

"You what, Val? Don't you remember telling me once that you weren't good with lies? That you couldn't keep your story straight and it was better to tell the truth?"

I slammed my eyes shut, remembering all too well how honest we had been with each other... as well as why everything had changed in a heartbeat. Angry at him for backing me up against a wall this way, I lifted my arms and pushed at his shoulders. The move was unsuccessful as he tightened his grasp on my waist and stepped forward until my back hit the literal wall. When I opened my eyes, our lips were mere inches apart.

"Please, Banner." I didn't know what else to do except plead, because even though I told myself otherwise, I couldn't bring myself to admit the baby was his out loud. It was shitty. *I* was shitty, but his heart was already broken by my marrying Sam.

No matter what I said or did in this moment, nothing would ever change the facts.

There were plenty of questions I could have asked, such as if he knew, why wouldn't he say something before now? Before today? Or when we first stood in that hotel doorway and told him the fake story?

But, I didn't as we stared at each other. "Please, Banner. I don't want Sam to find you in here holding me like this. Please go."

"Dammit, Val. Why would you do this? "His breath tingled against my mouth as he spoke. "I know you're afraid and you always have been, but we could have made it work if only you'd have given us the chance."

"Even if that were anywhere near the truth, it's too late now." Tears streamed down my cheeks because I had no defense against him in this moment. "I'm sorry, but you have to go."

"I will," he said, not moving, the pad of his thumb

caressing my lips as he gazed right into my eyes. "Just one last kiss, sweetheart, before I go because I want to make sure you understand what you've left behind."

He devoured my mouth with his, but it wasn't necessary. I knew what I was leaving behind, and I wouldn't ever forget, because my heart never let me through all these years. Everything about him was forever imprinted on every part of me, inside and out. No amount of distance would ever put either of us out of our mutual misery.

There was no point in fighting him, because I wanted this. I asked for it by keeping the truth from him, by marrying his best friend, and one day it would come back to bite me in the ass. Of that, I was positive.

The kiss was lustful and wanton, his hand digging into my waist as his other one left my face and traveled to my ass. He lifted me until my legs wrapped around his body. My guilt allowed him to take things further than a sweet innocent kiss. And I wanted to die from the pleasure of having his hands and mouth on me once again.

We feasted on one another because we both knew nothing and nobody else would ever fill the holes in each other as well as we did. Which meant this end was probably just another beginning like all the other times.

Tears streamed down my face when he pulled away. I cried harder when he moved enough to slide his hand around to rest on my stomach, staring into my eyes. "You and I know the truth, Val, and that's what matters to me."

Then, he lowered me to the ground slowly, kissed my forehead, and left the room without another word.

As for me, I waited for my hands and knees to stop shaking. Then I smoothed my clothing, made sure all signs of our kisses were gone from my face, and went to find Sam so he could get us both the hell out of here.

LATER THAT EVENING, I WENT THROUGH MY THINGS, finding a place for them among Sam's stuff. We moved everything from my parents' house earlier in the week, although tonight would be the first night I spent with him in the same bed. But even though it neared midnight, I couldn't relax enough to prepare for what would come from lying next to Sam.

I wanted to have sex with him, to explore the way his kiss earlier in the day made me feel. Yet something held me back and I didn't have to guess at what it might be.

Trying to shove him out of my mind despite what happened earlier, I smiled bright when Sam came into the bedroom. His hands were high in the air as he stretched his back, the move baring his flat and sexy six pack abs. Surprising as it might be, this moment was the first time he gave me a glimpse of what lay beneath his suits.

Shutting the drawer, I leaned back against the dresser and laughed as he stalked toward me, taking off his shirt in the process. Couldn't help my gaze dropping to his bare chest, especially when he stopped in front of me, grabbed me by the hips, and yanked me close enough to claim a kiss.

We didn't talk. Not after all the waiting and wondering.

My hands slid up his chest, onto his shoulders, and then up in the air as his hands found the edge of my shirt I changed into after the reception. He lifted it up and over my head. My arms came back down where I wrapped them around his neck as he continued kissing me. While deepening the connection of our lips, he began fondling my breasts through my bra.

There were only sighs and gasps from that moment on, as the rest of my clothing and his fell to the floor. Then we were on the bed, limbs and lips intertwined.

He did everything right.

There wasn't a moment's hesitation, or a missed opportunity for him to make me feel good — and vice versa — and we fit together nicely.

Well enough I could weep from the joy of it.

I should've been happy to have married someone I would have a fulfilling sex life with considering that had been my problem for years when it came to dating and sex, right?

So why did I have to force the lump down in my throat and take a deep breath to keep from crying as he snuggled me from behind once we finished? More so when he moved his hand to rest on my stomach, kissed my neck, and gently asked, "All right, love?"

Even in the most tender of moments like that, I couldn't get Banner out of my head. Images flashed through my mind of the night we spent in Paris together, and it made me angry.

At him

At myself.

At everything.

I made my bed. Why couldn't the world let me lay in it without the constant reminders of everything I could have if only I weren't such a coward?

Seriously, what the fuck was wrong with me?

Hadn't I made things hard enough on myself already?

I needed to stop it all. Stop thinking about him, wanting him, and wishing things were different between us.

Despite the fact he knew the truth.

How long had he known? And why hadn't he said something before I married Sam?

Then again, none of that mattered.

The fact was, nothing would've stopped me from doing anything I could to avoid having to admit the whole sordid story out loud to my family. I married Sam because I wanted to, because it was a perfect excuse to pretend Banner and I hadn't slept together.

That I wasn't in love with him.

Because, fuck yes, I was — and always had been — madly in love with him for far too long. Crazy, considering there wasn't any chance for us, nor would there likely ever be one.

Especially now.

The time had come to grow up and be a good mother to this child. Also be a good wife to the man lying behind me in bed, softly snoring since he passed out waiting for me to answer him.

Yeah.

Come morning, I would tell him everything was perfect. I was determined to push Banner from my mind to focus on the family I had now chosen and would protect at all costs.

With that, I sighed, snuggled in closer to Sam, and fell asleep seconds later into a dreamless slumber, for once.

October 4th

"Love, have you seen my keys?"

I laughed at Sam's question. He asked this almost daily because he never seemed to remember where he put his damned keys. And as usual, I called out from my seat on the cushy couch in the living room. "They're where they always are, in the hallway on the hooks!"

There was silence for a moment, then he strode into the room, a chagrined smile on his face as he leaned down to kiss me goodbye with his keys in hand. "You're right. You would think after two months, I would realize you've hanged them up before asking where they've gone to."

My heart fluttered when his lips met mine, my stomach clenching in anticipation. Nothing would happen because he needed to go and would be gone most of the day, but I loved his kisses and wanted more.

"I'll see you later, darling." He pulled away, moved to kiss my forehead, and just like that, I was alone.

Well, not so alone, as the baby suddenly kicked, and I laughed from the pure joy of it.

I never knew what a joy being pregnant would be. What I looked forward to more than anything was holding my baby in my arms. To loving him or her more than anyone else in my life.

And right now, Sam and this baby were all I had. We had finally decided to move to the UK, to live there as a family, and in truth, I was ready to get far away from this place.

I saw my friends occasionally, but both Macy and Sarah were still young and carefree. Neither were interested in marriage or children at this point and although we hung out every now and then, it wasn't the same as in the past. My life was boring now and I preferred it that way.

Sam loved me and yes, I loved him, for more than his decision to marry me and give the baby a family. I loved him for his kindness, the way he treated me well, and his never-ending patience. After the whirlwind way being with Banner made me feel, Sam's maturity and steadfastness made for a wonderful change. Both for my heart and the pace of my life, which had slowed down quite a bit.

Now I just waited to become a mother, filled my time up with hobbies, and tried not to worry so much about the future unless it involved my life with Sam.

But the ache for Banner never went away, especially every time the baby kicked because it reminded me of him. And despite all the new hope I had for the future, one moment was all it took for everything to come crashing down around every single of us.

For me to realize I had done nothing except fight the inevitable. That I wasted precious time with a man who would always love me, no matter how many times I pushed him away.

CHAPTER 14

DECEMBER 17TH

"HE'S BOUGHT ME OUT."

Sam spoke from behind me as I stood in the kitchen, making breakfast, and I turned at the dismay in his voice. "Can he do that?"

"Yes." He stood there, mouth agape, staring at some papers in his hand, and then he laughed, loud and boisterous. "Goddamn, it's a check for my initial investment, interest, and the buyout fee. How the feck did he manage that?"

"Let me see." I held out my hand, unable to believe Banner would do that out of nowhere. My own eyes popped when he walked over and placed the check in my hand. "Oh, wow, that's a lot of zeros."

Yes, I knew Sam was rich, but holy shit! There wasn't any way I could spend that money in two lifetimes, let alone one. I handed it back to him. "Did you know he was going to do this?"

"Nah. He never even hinted. He's worked with me as if nothing happened. That fucker." He chuckled again and folded the check in half, taking his wallet out to place it inside. "I'm going to call him up, love. Call if you need anything, all right?"

"You know I will."

At that, he stepped closer, let out a whoop, and whirled me around for a moment. Well, as best he could considering how my stomach stood out now. I had to laugh because this sort of cheerfulness was typical for him and it made our relationship easy. He was happy to make me happy and despite the way things began, I had married a good man five months ago.

When he finally let go, he kissed me quick and disappeared into his home office, shutting the door behind him.

Some days, I found it hard to believe this life was mine, in a good way.

To start, there wasn't any contact with Banner, at all. Sam continued to deal with him, but I never saw him or spent time with him. And it didn't seem as if he told Sam he knew about the baby being his. If anything, I took his comment in the room that day to mean he wouldn't interfere even though he would have to walk away from his child.

And it made me aware of exactly how much Banner loved me; to allow someone else to claim his child because I didn't dare admit the truth to our family for fear of losing them.

That's truly what it was. I didn't want to lose my family. I didn't want to look at me in disgust or disappointment and wonder how the hell they managed to raise someone like me, who would have sex with her cousin. Who cared if it was okay elsewhere? In America, it was weird and looked down upon and not something most people would accept. I didn't want my child raised around people who knew that truth, who would have issues with them for something they couldn't help.

That wasn't all though.

No, I had considered this a lot in the past five months while Sam and I stayed in his penthouse here in the States while. We were waiting on my visa to live in England with him as his wife.

And the truth was, nobody would have understood how I could continue to want Banner, need him, this man related to me.

They wouldn't understand how I couldn't just turn off my feelings, my attraction to him. How my heart beat faster when he looked at me and when he touched me. The way my breath caught when he put his hands on my cheeks and softly pressed his lips against mine. How could they get it when they had never experienced it?

Even while my life with Sam was pretty great, I did hate myself a tiny bit for walking away from Banner that morning after we slept together. Never had I ever wanted to hurt another person like I hurt him and this whole experience killed him as it had me for many years.

We were both paying for feeling something that wouldn't die regardless of who we were to each other.

And because of that day when I got married, I knew the real reason Banner bought out Sam. He wanted us gone from his lives completely; who could blame him?

Not me.

After all, Sam had me, the woman Banner wanted enough to kiss her right after she married someone else, and the child inside me he would raise as his own.

No, if anyone here was to blame, it was me, and I accepted that fact without a fight.

I wished that would get me to stop thinking of him, however. He was never far from my mind.

Hell, every time the baby kicked, all I could think of was him, for obvious reasons.

At that, I jerked out of my reverie and put a hand on my stomach, unable to recall if the baby had kicked in the last twenty-four hours. Yesterday morning is the last time I remembered. It wasn't something I typically thought about... just kind of side-noted in my brain because a baby should kick so often a day.

Unease creeping in, I took a couple deep breaths in

and out to stay calm. Then I stood quite still, resting a hand on my stomach while trying to see if the baby would move.

I poked at my stomach. Typically, when I did it in a certain spot, the baby's foot would respond to the stimuli and kick me, but again, nothing.

And that's when I began to worry.

Being due any day, I'd been waiting for my water to break, but suddenly, I had the urge to go to the hospital.

I waddled over to Sam's office door, knocked once, and then swung the door open to find him just hanging up the phone.

His smile died at what must've been the panicked expression on my face and completely wilted when I barely managed to say, "I think something's wrong with the baby."

That was the fastest I'd seen him move since the day we met.

* * *

I couldn't believe it.

The doctor spoke, Sam held my hand, but I couldn't hear anything. It was all noise after an emergency c-section when the doctor couldn't find a heartbeat. Where my sweet, beautiful little baby girl arrived into this world even though she would never take a breath of her own.

When they let me hold her, the perfect little creature whose eyes I would never see, I cried harder than ever before in my life until no more tears would come. That's when I let them take her away.

Sam had no words. In truth, there weren't any he could say that would make me feel better, so I was glad he didn't even try.

Although he wasn't able to crawl into bed with me to comfort me due to my surgery, he rarely left my side while I stayed in the hospital for three days.

I never spoke the entire time.

What could I say?

In my mind, her being stillborn was my fault and nobody could tell me anything else. If I were rational, I would've realized that, but I was as far from rational as a person could get.

And until the day I died, it was something I would never forget.

CHAPTER 15

FEBRUARY 17TH

Things changed between me and Sam after I returned home from the hospital.

A part of me always knew he married me because of the baby and what he thought knowing would do to Banner.

Who were we without having the thing we got together for?

I didn't know.

He called our family and friends to deliver the news when I refused to acknowledge what happened out loud.

I had no idea whether he told Banner or not, considering the buyout and everything. I didn't ask. I wouldn't ask, really, because I wouldn't speak.

For days after, I sat in the nursery, in the rocking chair we had gotten for when the baby arrived. Unless it was time to eat, I didn't want to do anything else.

By the fifth day, Sam had to carry me to the shower because it was the only way to ensure I would do it. Each time, I would spend the entire fifteen minutes sobbing as he scrubbed me clean.

He tried to talk to me, comfort me. Nothing penetrated the haze I lived in.

I couldn't work and ate only because I knew what kind of trouble would start if I didn't.

Sam never grew frustrated, however.

Today he entered the nursery and crouched down beside the chair. Placing one hand on my knee, he softly said, "Someone's here to see you."

I heard him, barely, but enough to mutter, my voice raw from all the crying. "I don't want to see anyone."

"You'll want to see him."

He rose without another word.

Before I could summon up the energy to insist I didn't, a familiar body knelt in front of me, hands on both my knees. I lifted my head up on gasp, my heart giving a little lurch at the sight of Banner's face right in front of mine.

It was the first emotion other than immense pain I experienced since the hospital.

"Hello, sweetheart." His greeting accompanied a sad smile. "I'm here to take you home."

And just like that, my short-lived marriage to Sam ended as Banner carried me out of the room.

July 28th

"How are you feeling?"

I stared at the therapist and shrugged, unable to answer the question.

Okay, more like I wasn't willing to, because even after six months of sessions, I couldn't manage to summon much emotion about anything.

The visits started right after Banner took me home.

For some reason, I thought he meant his place, but that had been foolish. By the end of the day he came to get me, I was back at my parents in my old room, where they hovered close by to check up on me every five minutes.

Apparently, Sam had expressed concern over my state of mind and knew the only person I might respond to would be Banner, hence him showing up that day.

And I had.

Only Banner did it for my family, not me.

They wanted me home, especially since Sam believed our marriage would never recover, and he wasn't wrong.

I married him for what I thought was all the right reasons at the time, except now it was clear they hadn't been. I tried to avoid drama and look where that got me.

Sitting here with a therapist, trying to move through the stages of grief so I could get on with my life.

Yeah right. I couldn't even manage to talk about the real problem... which would be me.

I remained stuck in denial. Unable to believe it happened and waiting, waiting, waiting for the horrible nightmare to end.

Surely this wasn't my life. How could I lose my own child? Was it something I did or didn't do at the beginning of the pregnancy?

The doctor told me it happened, that I didn't do anything wrong. The cord wasn't even around her neck when they delivered her. She would just... never take a breath.

But how could that be?

How could she grow so well, the pregnancy be easy and without anything going wrong, and yet, around the time she was due to arrive, just fucking not make it?

How fucking cruel.

Why would I want to acknowledge such a horrible tragedy was real?

"You should talk to him, Valerie," my therapist said, completely ignoring the fact I never answered her question, as she was used to me by now. "He's waiting for you to talk to him."

She spoke of Banner. He was the one brought me to these sessions and sat outside, waiting for me to finish so he could take me back to my parent's house.

Why did he waste his time?

How could he care so much he would push aside his hurt to take care of me, after I married another man while pregnant with his child?

And why did my heart have to pound every time I saw him, even after everything we'd been through?

I tried so hard to end things with him. For our relationship to be over for good.

Now that seemed like a mere waste of time since no matter how hard I tried, we always ended up together in one way or another.

On the way home from the session, he stayed silent as always.

Typically, I would too, but today, I wasn't quite ready to return to my parent's house yet. So, I reached over, covered his hand resting on the gear shift with mine, and quietly said, "I'm not ready to go home."

It was the first time I'd said a word to him in all these months and the feel of my hand on his must've been surprising, because the car swerved. He maneuvered the car back into its lane instantly. His gaze flicked toward me for a second before he merely cleared his throat and nodded to acknowledge my statement.

Removing my hand, I retreated to my side, curled my hand into a fist, and stared out the window for the rest of the drive.

He ended up taking me to his place.

On the way up, he walked behind me and after

unlocking the door, he swung it open to let me pass. Inside, he would hardly look at me as he said, "You're exhausted. Perhaps you should take a nap while I take care of a few things."

I wasn't going to argue because tired didn't even begin to explain how I felt all the time. He walked into the room I knew he used as his office while I headed toward the bedrooms.

There were three bedrooms, technically — one he used for an office, a guest bedroom, and his bedroom. Of course, I went into his bedroom and snuggled beneath the blankets. The familiar surroundings of the room comforted me in a way I hadn't been in three-fourths of a year.

I fell asleep to the sound of chirping outside the windows and it was the deepest I'd slept in what felt like a lifetime.

CHAPTER 16

JULY 29TH

THE RAISED VOICES OF BANNER AND SYLVIA RIGHT outside the bedroom door woke me up.

"What is she doing here?"

"Please keep your voice down."

Their voices grew a bit fainter, as if they moved down the hallway, so I crept out of bed to stand closer to the door, which I had left cracked a little.

"I'll fucking raise my voice if I want to," she snapped at him. "How dare you bring her here!"

Banner's voice had calmed, quieted in tone, and the way he said, "She's been through a lot," in reply made my heart twinge a bit.

"Oh, for feck's sake. We've all been through a lot this year, Brad. I feel for her, I really do as I can't imagine losing a child, but she isn't your responsibility in the slightest."

I couldn't tell by the conversation whether she knew or not about Banner's role in the pregnancy. Then again, why would he tell her or anyone, considering everybody assumed the baby was Sam's, as I wanted them to?

"She's my family, Sylvia."

"Oh, thank you for telling me that. I wasn't aware." Her voice dripped with sarcasm and I wondered how Banner could be with someone like her. "This happens to be your cousin who married your business partner? The one you then bought out for reasons I'm still not certain of? The one we postponed our wedding for because she lost the baby a month before we were to get married."

Ah, that's why she's angry. Banner put me before his fiancée's desires and she's more pissed over that than my presence here today.

"It's been six months since then, Brad. When do we get on with our life together, of marrying and having our own family?" She sniffles before tacking on, "I'm not getting any younger you know. I want a child with you sooner than later."

When Banner finally speaks, it's with a resignation I've heard from him only a few times before. This wasn't going to end well for her. "I'm sorry, Sylvia. I'm afraid that isn't going to happen."

"Pardon?" The question was a screech, an unwillingness to accept what he's said without a blunt statement. "What isn't going to happen?"

"We're not getting married Sylvia." He paused and then delicately added, "I love her and she is my concern because that child was mine."

I couldn't breathe, astonished at him admitting the truth out loud like that, out of nowhere. I had expected him to say what he said before in more pointed terms. I didn't expect him to tell her that, especially considering he had no idea if I felt the same damn way about him anymore.

That's when the cursing started. Then a slap echoed down the hall, no doubt delivered from her and even I thought he deserved it for telling her that way. Basically, he lied to her the entire time because he knew and only now did he tell her, instead of letting her decide if she wanted to stay with someone having a child with another woman.

It wasn't before long the door downstairs slammed closed. When I opened the bedroom door to announce my presence, he stood frozen in the spot down the hall, hand on his cheek.

Didn't turn to face me as he acknowledged me by asking, "Feeling better?"

I answered him with a laugh. "What the fuck were you thinking?"

"She was my best friend for a long time." His sigh was sad sounding. "I quickly realized she wasn't the woman I wanted to marry not long after we became engaged."

"So why didn't you tell her that?"

"I was going to until she dragged me into that damn engagement party, which she set up without me knowing. Then I saw you standing there next to that damn booth with Sam, of all the damn people in the world."

"Wow." I laughed but it's the kind filled with incredulity. "Are you blaming me for you two not separating?"

He stalked toward me then, stopping when we were inches apart. I could feel the heat from his body, desired for him to lay his hands on me for even a moment as he hissed, "Yes. That story you two concocted was bullshit. I couldn't imagine the agony of loving another woman who would do something like that to me, because you were incapable of doing the right thing at the time. Sylvia would never have done such a thing."

"Oh, fuck you, Banner." Stepping back, I crossed my arms over my chest and scowled, refusing to acknowledge his second declaration of love in a matter of minutes. "I came to tell you about the baby that day. You're the idiot who got engaged barely three months after fucking me in Paris. What the hell did you expect me to do when I found that out?"

He didn't even flinch. "Still tell me the truth, for starters."

"And what? Break your heart? Tear apart your engagement when we both knew I would never would allow us to get together?" I scoffed and shook my head.

"You just don't get it, do you? I was trying to make sure you were happy."

"And when will you fucking realize," he seethed, stepping inside the room and shutting the door behind him, "that you're the only fucking woman in the world who will ever make me happy?"

"You're a hopeless romantic, Banner, and I'm a hardcore realist." My laugh sounded empty, hollow, and heartless. "It'll never work out."

"Because you won't let it."

"No!" I shouted now, my entire body shaking and my palms sweating, unprepared as I was for this conversation. "Because it's the truth. Because it's always been the truth. Because I deliberately kept the facts about the child from you, Banner. I can't be trusted. My words, my heart, they can't be trusted to do the right thing if it will in any way affect my relationship with my family."

"I'm your family!" He shouted back at me, stalking over to me and backing me up until my knees hit the edge of the bed and I sat down on it. "That's why you need to stop with the bullshit excuses, Val. I'm your fucking family and you've got no issue with hurting me as often as you goddamn please."

"The fact you're my family is the entire fucking problem."

Silence.

Complete, utter silence as he stood before me, above

me, staring down with utter desperation in his eyes, fists hanging at his sides.

Until he said, through clenched teeth, "I don't care, Val. I won't let you use that as an excuse anymore. Fuck the consequences. You're a goddamned adult and you need to act like one."

This time, faced with his wrath and despair, I became the one to crack, so fucking tired of fighting against the one thing I wanted. The world didn't care about hurting me, so why did I care so much about taking what I wanted while I could have it?

"I tried." Tears began streaming down my face, my despair finally breaking free after all these months of being trapped inside me. "I tried so hard to be an adult, to spare us both from pain, and all I've done is the opposite. Our daughter..."

It was the first time I said those two words out loud; it was like me flicking a switch from one position to the other. Banner swooped in, forcing me to lay back on the bed as his mouth ravaged my lips and his body trapped mine beneath his.

After a few minutes of deep, passionate kissing, he released my lips long enough to say, "The news broke my heart. I would've been there for you, if I could've been."

"I know."

"Stop hurting me, Val. Nothing in this world will keep

me from loving you, this has fucking shown that. All this crap? The back and forth? It needs to end."

How could I keep doing this? I couldn't. When would enough be enough? Continuing to hurt the one person who loved me no matter what didn't make sense.

Sniffling, I sank further into his hold, grabbing his shirt tightly in my fists as I whispered, "I'm sorry. I'm afraid. I've always been afraid of the repercussions. That people won't understand."

"So, what? Do you know how fucking tortured I've been, for no goddamn reason?" He kissed me again after I shook my head. "I never forget anything. The smell of your hair, the taste of your skin. Every time you walk away, I'm left with your imprint all over my life and by the time I've managed to rid myself of you... god, there you are. Back again, turning everything inside out so nothing makes sense once more and I'm wondering why the hell I let you do this to me. To us. Over and over. It has to stop. We need to pick this side and stick with it, no matter how hard it is. Or how hard it becomes."

"How?" I had to force the word past my lips, stuttering through my sobs. "How will I admit the truth... tell my family what really happened? They'll never trust me again."

"Why the hell do you think that?"

"Because it's true."

"There's no way to know that. You're the only person

I've met in my entire life who hates herself enough to screw up her whole life all in the name of loving and protecting others."

Of course, he was right. I fell in love with him and had hated myself for it ever since. "I know. How can you not hate me after what I've done?"

"I could never hate you." He kissed me quick and smirk. "I know that for a fact because I tried and look where we are. In my bed, where I want to do anything and everything except let you leave me again."

"Oh, god." My eyes welled up again and more tears slipped down my cheeks as I told him something he should've heard a long time ago. "I love you so much it hurts."

"I love you, too, Val."

With that, he rolled off me, readjusted our positions on the bed so we could get under the blankets, and crawled in to snuggle me from behind.

"You'll stay the night?"

Too tired and raw to argue, I yawned, weakly nodding as I snuggled into the pillow. "Yeah."

"We'll figure everything out, Val. I promise, it'll be okay."

It wasn't the first time he said those words, made that promise. Yet, somehow, all these years later... I believed him this time, and fell asleep with a little hope back in my heart.

CHAPTER 17

JULY 31ST

My parents were the first people who heard the true story.

When we entered the house, I went first and Banner came in behind me. He wanted to hold my hand but I wouldn't let him.

"We should tell them first," I had told him. "It would be weird to just show up that way, don't you think?"

He didn't agree. We were going to tell them either way, was his argument. In the end, I got my way though because every time he went to take my hand in his, I would move it out of his reach.

Since I spent the last three nights at his place — and came home every morning after — I went into my bedroom to change as he and my parents took a seat in the living room.

I told my mother I'd been spending the night with a friend. At this point, she hadn't questioned anything, because she was happy about me doing anything that didn't involve hiding in my room all day.

"Been a while since we've seen you, Banner," my mother was saying as I finally entered the living room. "How have you been?"

"Good."

When I sat beside him, he reached over and snatched my hand before I had a chance to hide it.

My mother's eyes about popped out of her skull as she asked, "What is going on?"

"There's something you should know, Aunt Rose." He glanced my way and kept his eyes on me as he said, "I'm in love with your daughter."

Trust Banner to just blurt it out like that.

"But—" my mother started to interject, while my father merely sat beside her stroking his newly grown beard, face neutral.

Of course, Banner wasn't going to give them a chance to think about all the implications for long. He jumped into when he and I first met in that club, how we kissed outside without knowing who each other were. He told them all about not knowing about our relation. Him because he used Brad instead of the name I always knew him as, and me because I told him my name was Anne.

My mother actually glared at me for a moment when

he said that, but man, he was terrific at gaining her attention again. He made sure to explain we hadn't any idea about being cousins until the day they showed up to tell us about his father's death.

And the more he carried on, basically telling them everything – including how he had been the father of the baby – the more I wanted to crawl into a hole to die at the look of complete devastation on my mother's face.

When he finally stopped talking, she didn't even give me a chance to say anything. She stood up and strode out of the room. My father followed her a moment after, although his expressionless face gave nothing away about his feelings over the situation.

I sobbed.

Rising, I yanked my hand from Banner's and ran from the room, then straight out the front door, convinced my parents would never, ever talk to me again.

❧

"Val?"

My gaze remained locked on the sights outside the window, my chin in my hand while my elbow rested on the windowpane. I occasionally swiped at the tears sliding down my cheeks as I replied to Banner's utterance. "Yeah?"

"Dinner's ready."

"That's nice."

Eating was the last thing on my mind.

A whole four days had passed since we went to my parents' place and I hadn't heard a word from them since. The fact they wouldn't even acknowledge my presence the day after broke my heart. I ended up packing up my things and moving into Banner's because their silence had become unbearable.

"You need to eat, Val."

"No, I don't."

I wished he would go away. The past few days, he went to work for a few hours, but he would return soon after. He kept trying to get me to do something like eat or go outside all in the name of being worried about me.

Stupid.

The fact he talked me into telling my parents was the whole reason I acted in a way that made him worry about me. He told me everything would be okay but it wasn't and I had no way to know if it ever would be again.

"I'm sorry," he said softly, the apology sudden and unexpected. "For the fact they reacted that way. I should've listened to you about them."

"You're sorry?" I sniffled, swiped at the tears on my face, and faced him with furrowed brows. "Too late for that. Who knows if they'll ever speak to me again."

"They will, Val. They're your parents and they love you."

"Oh, bullshit."

The emotion in his face cooled as he slipped his hands into his pockets and frowned. "Fine. You want my thoughts on their behavior?"

"Yeah, please. Don't feed me crap."

"They're assholes," he stated bluntly. "You're their daughter and they do love you, but they love their version of you. The one who has always done what they wanted her to do and not caused any trouble, never gave them any reason to worry. Sure, they could forgive you for the unplanned pregnancy, because you got married and 'fixed' it in their eyes, but now they know the truth. And they can't reconcile that with the person they've always pretended you were."

Even though I knew he was right in my heart, I surged to my feet and poked him in the chest, my whole body burning with indignation. "And how the fuck is that supposed to make me feel better?"

"It won't." His eyes softened, his right hand coming up to my face, where he stroked my cheek with the pad of him thumb. "They'll either get over it, sweetheart, or they won't. And all that does is make it clear their love for you is not unconditional."

I didn't have a response to that, but he didn't need one.

"Until then, you get on with your life. I'll do anything to see that beautiful smile I love so much on your face again."

And wasn't that the problem?

"I don't know how," I admitted.

He smiled at that. "I do."

Of course, he did. He wouldn't be him without understanding exactly how things in my life could go from this moment. Where everything had changed in the last year and a half to the point I no longer recognized my old one.

"First," he added, kissing my lips quickly before reaching down to take my hand in his, "we're eating dinner. Then, we're spending the evening together, doing whatever you want to do. And finally, you'll come sleep in my bed."

My lips quirked at that. "Oh, I will?"

I might've moved in, but like so many years ago when we spent a lot of time together upon first finding out who each other were, we hadn't had sex. I didn't even sleep in the same bed; upon taking the guest bedroom, he declared it my own personal space because he understood how much I needed that.

Sleep together in the same bed again, though? Was I ready for that, for where it could lead considering the last time?

"There are a lot of things you should think about, but this isn't one of them." His gaze was gentle while his voice firmed to let me know how serious this was to him.

"Thinking about it to the point of worrying is the opposite of what we both need you to do. After everything we've been through, this is our time. The right thing."

"You think so?"

"More than that. I know, with every bit of my heart, that you and I... we are the best for each other." He pressed a soft kiss against my lips and then released my hand, changing the subject while leaving me wanting more. "Now, let's eat. Please?"

"Okay."

I didn't agree because I felt hunger or because the smell of the food finally made me want to eat. I agreed for Banner, to release some of his own worry about me, and to help me let go of the heavy heat of anger in my heart at myself for disappointing my parents.

And that evening, after we finished dinner, we spent two hours watching comedy shows on Netflix. I spent the night snuggled into Banner's side, his left arm wrapped around my shoulders as a blanket covered us both.

Some parts, I laughed so hard I cried, and Banner wasn't far off from that either, wiping at his eyes when he thought I wasn't looking.

It felt nice, normal even, and not once did I think about my family or anything to do with all the things that kept us apart all these years.

For once, I really started to believe everything would

be okay, great even. When he kissed me that night, as we stood at the foot of his bed, all I wanted was more of the thing I hadn't had in way too long by that point — his touch.

My heart pounded as his tongue sought and won entry into my mouth. When his hands slid beneath my shirt and up my rib cage, his thumbs caressing the sensitive spot right beneath the curve of my breasts, covered by my bra. When they slipped around the back and he undid the hooks with little effort, my stomach flipped. As I stood topless in the dim light of the moonlight streaming in the window, he stared down at me with more than a gleam of appreciation in his eyes.

The only emotions coursing through me were love and the desire for Banner to be as exposed as I was, which is when I helped him out of his shirt as well. Not even a minute passed before we were both naked, standing in front of each other for the first time since Paris. When he lifted me into his arms, I went more than willingly toward an unknown future with a man who had never given up on me despite how many times he probably should have.

It was at this point where I chose our love and to live the life we were meant to have together, instead of being afraid of what everyone thought of us. Things felt too right as we kissed and touched, skin against skin, in his bed, more than they ever had before.

The moment to stop caring about everybody else except Banner was now.

Giving in meant if things didn't go well, I couldn't blame it on everybody else. On society. By saying it out loud, by coming out to my family — and his mother, who may know by now if my mother told her — there wasn't anything left to wonder about their reaction.

Were they sad or disgusted? I didn't know. All I knew was that they would either come around or they wouldn't. Either way, I had Banner, and if we lost each other, if we failed to live up to what we had honestly dreamed about, I didn't know what either of us would have left.

But I couldn't let fear stop me any longer, let the unknown be the scariest part of all. If I had realized this earlier, we would've had this for longer, instead of waiting until there wasn't any way we could deny our love and need for each other... after the world had gotten tired of our back and forth, making us pay for our decisions up to now.

And when our bodies joined once more, when he was as deep inside my body as he was my heart, I wrapped my arms around his neck. I buried my face there as the immense pleasure and joy wracked every inch of me. Then, after he finished and rolled over, taking me with him to hold in his arms, that's when I cried.

Finally when I allowed the grief over our child's death

to hit me once more, as I shared with him the pain and sorrow we both had held onto for so long.

He embraced me until there weren't any more tears to cry.

Then, he said the one thing I hadn't known I wanted to hear until that very moment, as he moved to cover my body so he could look down at my tear streaked face.

"Val, there's nothing more in the world I want with you than to have a family." His swiped at wetness on my cheeks, swooped in to kiss me long and soft, then whispered against my lips, "Do you want to try again?"

In spite of the instant anxiety that stuck my heart over every single bad thing that could happen, all the reasons I could think of to say no... I couldn't, because the decision had already been made. And the man above me, watching me with gentle and love-filled eyes, deserved to have everything with me that he could have with somebody else.

"I love you," I whispered, lifting a hand to cup his cheek and allowing the peace of letting what would be to wash over me before smiling. Happy tears pricked my eyes this time. "I want the same thing."

His reply came not in words, but in the grin on his face. The tension left his form as he brought his body back down on mine, all while muttering, "No time like the present to get started."

And for the next three days, we locked ourselves away

from the rest of the world, not caring about anything or anyone else other than each other.

Too bad the people who understood the least would intrude far sooner than we wished in the form of his mother and mine, teamed together for the first time in four decades.

CHAPTER 18

AUGUST 8TH

"You're kidding."

I shouldn't have opened the door, especially since Banner wasn't here. He left earlier to go to work since he hadn't been in all week thanks to me.

But why wouldn't I open the door when I saw my mother standing there through the peephole?

Of course, my thoughts were along the lines of she had come to apologize, to tell me she loved me despite my choices, but no. My aunt Judy stood off to the side, waiting for me to open the door before they both barged in. They told me to pack my things because there wasn't any way they were going to let this "disgusting thing" happen between me and Banner.

"Time to come home, Valerie." My mother ignored my comment and swiped up a stack of shirts from the dresser, shoving them into a bag she had brought along to assist. "You're coming with me."

I loved my mother. The part of me that didn't want to ignore her, to tell her no, was the good girl part of me Banner had referred to. The one who had never given her parents cause to worry or get upset with her; the one who hadn't been herself for so long because she didn't want to let them down.

But I wasn't letting them down by loving Banner. I had to keep telling myself that and not because I didn't believe it. No, because there wasn't anything wrong with loving him. Yet a lifetime of beliefs otherwise weren't easy to overcome, not when my mother stood before me practically begging me with her eyes not to fight with her about this.

"Stop!" She kept going even as I stood beside her and pulled things out as she put them in, tossing them wherever they would land in an attempt to make her quit. "I'm not coming home with you."

"This is sickening," Judy spat from behind me. "And the fact you two hid this from us? Unbelievable."

I whirled around and pointed at the door, my finger shaking. "Then get out. Nobody asked you to come here."

"Valerie! You will not speak to your aunt that way!"

"Oh, please." I turned back to my mother and grabbed at the bag, attempting to tug it from her tight grip. My chest burned with an emotion I couldn't pinpoint in that moment. "You two barely speak for most of your lives and now you want to act like you're the best of friends? Glad to see I've given you something to reunite over."

My mother huffed and straightened her shoulders, glaring at me like she did the other day at the house. "We've always had different opinions, Valerie, but we're sisters. In this, we agree. You are my daughter; he is her son. It isn't right."

There was a lump in my throat as my gaze flicked between my mother and my aunt, working up the guts to say what I needed to say next. I had to make them see what was going on, to accept it for what it was, for what they can't change. Also, to get them to leave before one of us said something we couldn't take back.

Eyes watering, I gestured around the room and focused on my mother. "Look around you, Mom. Don't you get it? Banner and I... we're together. Together, as in we are officially a couple."

"No, you are not." Her scowl deepened, her gaze holding onto mine almost painfully, refusing to acknowledge the nicely made bed to her left that I couldn't have possibly slept in last night because it wasn't even eight in the morning. "You're not well, Valerie. You made a bad decision, you lost... you lost the child. You need help."

"I'm fine, Mom." The words were a whisper, a soft begging for her to accept the truth before her and leave me be. "We love each other. Why can't you be happy for us, that we want to try again to have a family?"

"You are already family!"

The moment my mother shouted at me, I knew nothing I said would change her mind or ever allow her to see my relationship with Banner differently. My mother never raised her voice to me or stood before me looking at me as if I were a creature she didn't recognize.

Shaking my head, I turned around and stalked past Judy, standing by the door as I quietly said, "I need you to leave. Now."

"Valerie." It was Judy this time, putting her hand on my shoulder even though I refused to look at either of them, until she gave it a squeeze and said, "Please."

When I lifted my gaze, she gave a tight smile and said, "That's better. Now, we understand you're upset, but please try to see this from our side."

"Why? You refuse to see it from mine."

She didn't even flinch, her hand leaving my shoulder as she sighed. "Your mother told me everything. You believe I want unhappiness for my son? For you, my niece? No, darling, I want both of you to have a fulfilling, beautiful lives and my belief it isn't with each other doesn't mean I don't understand."

"No?"

"No. I love my son. He is all I have and I don't want to upset him. Just as your mother doesn't wish to upset you.

All we want you and him to do is understand how this isn't healthy for either of you. Perhaps a bit of it is our faults, as you two didn't get to spend time together growing up, but—"

Refusing to listen to this any longer, I shook my head and cut her off. "No. We're both adults and you two need to back off. We're not children. We don't need you telling us what we can and can't do, like we're stupid and have no idea what we want."

"Val—"

"No, Mom." I didn't look at her, couldn't bear to see the hurt in her eyes while I finally stood up for something I wanted no matter how much it also pained me. "I've made my decision and nothing you two or anybody else says is going to change my mind. You need to leave, please. Just go."

I thought she would continue to argue, leaving me no choice except to call Banner to help get them the hell out of here. But she surprised me by stating, "There's always a place for you at home, Valerie. When you've seen the mistake you've made and you're willing to no longer see or speak to him, your room will be waiting for your return."

They left after that, leaving me alone with my thoughts and my tears, but they were ones of anger, not sadness. My mother didn't consider me an adult. Rather she considered me a rebellious child who would come running home when things didn't work out with Banner as I thought they would.

And despite all my fears, all my worries — the ones that had kept me and Banner apart for too long — I became determined to ensure my future never involved returning home to a place where I was no longer understood.

❦

"IT'S GOOD TO SEE YOU, LOVE."

The familiar, friendly cadence of Sam's voice had me turning around from where I stood outside Banner's office waiting for him to return. I smiled at my now ex-husband as if we hadn't made a terrible decision to marry in the first place.

The good thing was the whole fiasco hadn't put an end to their friendship, only their business relationship. According to Banner, that had been an expected ending from the get go. Well, except it came a little sooner than anticipated, but I had merely been glad a lifelong affection hadn't gotten destroyed alongside everything else.

"Same to you, Sam." And it was true. He looked good as always, happy, standing there with both hands in his pockets and a grin on his face. "What are you doing here?"

"Waiting on lunch with my best mate." Stepping forward, he lifted one hand and caressed my cheek with his thumb, then scowled. "Have you been crying? Whose arse needs kicked, hmm?"

I thought nobody could see the result of this morning's run in with my mother and aunt, but guess not. "Nobody's ass, Sam. Let's just say our families didn't take the news so well."

"Oh." He glanced away for a moment, then back, his expression a little less happy as dropped his hand from my face. "I suppose you're here to tell him, then."

"Yeah. I mean, he probably already knows. I doubt his mother hasn't said something to him."

He laughed and shook his head. "Oh, she has. And me, as well."

"What?"

"Yeah, earlier this week. Told me to beg you to take me back, to promise you I would be a better husband. A bit insulting, innit?"

I laughed because he winked while saying it. "You were a great husband, but you know that already."

"Of course, love." He smirked and slipped his free hand back into his pocket. "Are things better?"

I appreciated him asking, even if he didn't get more specific, because we both knew what he meant. "Yes, thank you. We're... we're going to try again. Did he tell you that?"

Both his brows raised. "Perhaps that was the bit he wished to share at lunch."

"Oh."

He shook his head as I bit my lip, then leaned in to peck me on the cheek. "I'm happy for you two, love."

That is the moment Banner walked around the corner. Even though we weren't doing anything wrong, I jerked away from Sam when Banner said, "Are you hitting on my girlfriend, mate?"

Not that he was truly bothered, though, as they both laughed. Banner put his arm around my shoulders when he got close enough and kissed me on the lips before saying, "I'm sorry you had to wake up to that this morning."

"It's all right. Not really what I thought I would wake up to this morning but nothing I can do. They wouldn't listen."

"They'll come around, sweetheart."

Ah, how I wished he was correct, but something told me that once more, I was being the more realistic one out of the two of us. That my mother would never forgive me, which meant my father wouldn't either, because he always sided with my mother.

He said that's what kept their marriage strong — they always had each other's back, even if they disagreed in private. I knew that as long as my mother wasn't happy, my father wouldn't be either even if he might side with me otherwise.

It wasn't right, not at all, but it was their life, and this was mine. It wasn't compatible and probably never would be, yet there wasn't any other way. Neither of us would bend and so now, our relationship was broken, perhaps forever.

My heart hurt, the rift stinging, yet even standing here with Banner's arm around me, I felt safe. Comforted. Loved.

And that would have to be enough. I had him, my friends, and hopefully a family with Banner in the near future.

I focused on that as we headed to lunch together. I was ready to move on with my life while living on my own terms, and not once had I anticipated how much the world would continue to fuck with my dreams.

"Oh, wow, Val. The house looks amazing."

I stood to the side in the foyer, staring at Macy and Sarah, who both gazed wide eyed at the interior of my and Banner's new home.

In the six months since we finally got together, a lot had changed. Banner wanted more for us than only living together; he wanted to marry me. Since it wasn't legal for us in Ohio, we made the decision together to move to another state that did allow it. Although we didn't have to move — we could've gotten married in another state without residency requirements then returned home — the truth is, we both wanted and needed a fresh start.

We spent a month deciding on a state and then, we started looking at houses. That took a bit longer than I thought it should, but he had a particular idea for the kind of property he wanted. All I cared about was having a house with a yard that wasn't on a busy street, so he got to search for the perfect home that would fit both of us.

After he presented me with his choices, I was the one who made the final decision, and two months ago, this was the house he purchased. And when I say that, I mean that he wrote a check for the full amount — which ran into the hundreds of thousands — so we owned the house outright. Even though I knew Banner had a lot of money, considering how he bought out Sam, I couldn't deny being a little surprised at him writing that check. I knew a lot more about his finances now, though. Okay, "our finances" as he said, because he made it clear it's our money now.

Not that I cared. I wasn't used to having money at my disposal and it didn't change anything. However, to me, the house was worth every penny despite being more than I ever imagined spending on a house. Five bedrooms, two-and-a-half baths, sitting on ten beautiful acres of land in Virginia. The house wasn't too far of a drive from the ocean or a busy metropolitan area where we could shop, eat, and have fun together.

I smiled at my friends, happy at their pleasure with my house and nodded toward the rest of the house. "Come on, guys. I'll show you the rest of it."

"Sure, I would love that." Macy lifted a brow and put her hands on her hips, smirking at me. "But first, let's see that ring."

Even though they had seen plenty of pictures since

Banner asked me to marry him, they hadn't seen the ring in person because he just slipped one on my finger a few weeks ago.

It wasn't anything fancy. He knew me, so he wouldn't buy something I wouldn't like. Although the diamond ended up being a bit bigger than I would have chosen, I loved the simplicity of the ring as well as its meaning.

So, I held out my hand and they both squealed, Sarah taking my hand to take a closer look as Macy sighed.

"Gorgeous. Does he have any brothers?"

Her question made me and Sarah laugh, mostly because she already knew that answer. They also knew everything about Banner. They were the only people outside of my family who knew the truth and I preferred to keep it that way. Not because of shame or anything; it just didn't seem necessary for anyone to know except those closest to me.

Even more, they were terrific. They hadn't been revolted when I told them the truth, surprisingly. Yes, they shocked me, because I couldn't understand why they weren't as bothered by it as I was. That's when I found out Sarah had a cousin who married another of their cousins. She wasn't disgusted by it at all and even said the fact we didn't grow up together made it even less weird for her than when her own cousins did it.

Macy had just shrugged, said we can't help who we love, and ordered another drink that night. I had joined them, for the first time feeling like I wouldn't lose everyone important to me by choosing Banner. Those moments really helped me perceive my life in a different way.

I loved them, they loved me, and they also got to know Banner, so they loved him for me, as good friends should. He treated me well, which is all they cared about, and I appreciated it with all my heart.

Especially when they forgave me for not telling them the truth in the first place.

The best friends a girl could ask for. Truly.

"All right." Sarah dropped my hand and frantically searched around the corridor. "Where's the bathroom in this place?"

Macy laughed, I pointed down the hall to the left, and we giggled even harder when Sarah took off at a full run.

I had little doubt their visit would be fun. I couldn't wait for Banner to return in time for dinner so he, too, could share in an enjoyable evening at home with me and my best friends at what was now one of the happiest times of my life.

BANNER ENTERED THE DINING ROOM AND LAUGHED while unbuttoning his sleeves to roll them up. "I see you three couldn't wait for me to join you before indulging yourselves with the wine."

"Here. Let me pour you some." I picked up a glass and tipped the bottle, a little pouring onto the table before I corrected myself, giggling. "How much do you want?"

"I'll do it." With a quick kiss on my lips, he sat beside me and gently removed both the bottle as well as the glass from my hands. "The fact you're drunk tells me this is the second bottle, not the first."

My friends, having had as much to drink as I had, snickered and set their now empty glasses on the table.

"We're only drunk because instead of eating, we waited for you." Macy stuck her tongue out and reached for her fork. "I don't know about you, but I'm starving."

"Okay, okay." Banner took a few sips from his glass and set it on the table, then stood up again, his gaze flicking between the three of us. "Any of you able to help bring the food to the table?"

I rose from my seat slowly, grinning at him. "I can do it. I didn't really drink so much wine that I can't walk."

"All right."

He let me lead the way into the kitchen, walking closely behind me in case I misjudged my wine intake enough to trip or something. Once the door shut behind us, he grabbed me around the waist. Turning me in his arms, our mouths met a second later, his devouring mine as if he couldn't get enough of me.

The truth was, I couldn't get enough of him either.

From the moment we were together again, every day

had been like this, barring those few days a month where we didn't. We'd even christened many, many surfaces in the new house since moving in, and it's been amazing every single time. I thought it would wane — everyone always says it slows down after a while, even my friends — so I don't take any moments with him for granted.

Now, however, wasn't the time to start something neither of us could finish; not when my friends were waiting to eat. When I began to pull back, he groaned and held me tighter, kissing me for a few moments longer before drawing away, muttering, "I swear I'll never get enough of you."

"Ditto." Pecking his cheek, I stepped back and turned toward the oven. "Let's eat before they both start to riot. You know how they get when they're hungry."

He smacked my ass, chuckled when I let out a squeak, and then helped me carry the food to the table.

The evening passed in a blur as we all drank too much wine, my friends regaled us both with their recent dating stories, and I tried not to think about how my family wouldn't be there tomorrow to see Banner and I get married.

When my thoughts did wander that way, I looked around the table, chose to be grateful for the wonderful people that were in my life, and focused on them.

I was happy, after all, and for once, I let my own happiness be the only thing that mattered.

CHAPTER 20

FEBRUARY 9TH

"Beautiful."

Sam leaned against the doorjamb, hands in his suit pockets and grinning as I stood in front of the mirror, giving myself a once over before heading down to marry Banner.

Although we hadn't been sure Sam would show up now that he was running the casino back in Ohio, my breath let out in a little sigh of relief at his presence.

He had been a constant through everything; both Banner and I considered Sam my friend as well as his.

"Thank you."

Stepping inside, he shut the door and stalked toward me, pulling me into a tight hug as he laughed. "I was referring to the house."

I rolled my eyes as he released me. "Asshat."

"No, love." He grabbed my bare upper arms, gazing

into my eyes with his own, all his affection for me clear in them. "There are no words to describe how stunning you are in this moment. It would be a scandal to merely say you look beautiful."

Even though I blushed at words, I knew he truly meant them and tears pricked my eyes. "You're sweet."

"Ah, ah." He shook his head and released my arms. "Dry those tears, darling. You've a wedding to attend and I don't need another punch to the face. Especially when there are such gorgeous creatures' downstairs in your living room."

"Ha! Those are my friends. My best friends, Macy and Sarah." I wiggled my finger in his face playfully. "I'll need you to keep your hands to yourself."

"Promise." He crossed his fingers and winked. "But only until after the reception, then all bets are off."

"Sam!"

I didn't know if he was serious. Not that it mattered. Sam was a good man and had been the kind of husband any woman would want; he deserved happiness. If it happened with one of my friends, I would be glad for them. Why not when they would be with a man who truly cared for the woman he was with?

And as I stood there next to my ex-husband while preparing to marry the man I should've married instead, there was an unanswered question I needed to ask.

He made it about Banner the first time. Something I

chose to believe at the time even though we both knew better, that it hadn't been about him at all.

I needed to hear the truth. The *real* reason behind a marriage that held me together at a time I needed it the most despite not recognizing that fact. "Why did you do it, Sam? Why did you marry me?"

"Because you weren't ready, love."

Even though I had an idea of what he referred to, I still wanted him to say it anyway. "For what?"

"To risk everything for him. And he knew it as well."

Right. There it was, the real reason.

Even so, remembering the fight I had with Banner after he ended things with Sylvia months ago, my cheeks flushed at recalling how angry he had been. My confusion grew. "So, that was a test? He wanted to see if I would tell him the truth or choose you instead?"

"I wouldn't put it like that, love. Angry or not, he was adamant you have a choice over what happened next."

"What does that mean? He let me marry you?"

"Yes. Before you woke up in that room, he knew you were pregnant and the child was his. He also understood even if you told him, you weren't ready to build a life together, to risk telling your family the truth."

Not expecting to have it confirmed that Banner knew the truth from the beginning, my mouth dropped open. "But he punched you!"

Sam laughed. "He did. I'm afraid it was all for show,

although he hadn't been completely sure you would accept my proposal. Hell, I was convinced you would turn me down flat."

"W...what? Why would he want you to marry me? And why would you want to?"

"Because we're best mates, love. You were better off with someone he trusted, someone who would let him see the child even if his role was more similar to an uncle. And I'm a stupid Englishman who has a thing for attractive, smart, American women."

Perhaps this news should've made me angry, as well as Sam's avoidance in answering why he wanted to marry me. All I remembered was how Banner seemed to avoid us after we got married. However, that wasn't the truth at all. Sam said I wouldn't have to see him if I didn't want to and that's what happened. I chose not to see Banner, chose to marry Sam, and chose to hide the truth.

And Banner accepted my decisions, even if they hurt him, even if they kept him from knowing his child as a father. Not that it explained everything.

"Then he kissed me after the wedding...?"

"Ah, yes. Earned a shiner for that after he fessed up." Sam chuckled at my frown. "Don't look so sad, darling. I loved you, I did, yet you would never love anyone as you did him and after you lost the child, I knew you wouldn't stay with me. You needed him, especially then, and he needed you."

"You're right." I hated that he was correct, but considering I stood here now, ready and eager to marry Banner, there wasn't any denying it. He was the love of my life and Sam, for all the ways he tried to help, would never have been enough in the end. "Thank you for telling me."

The rest of my thoughts, I didn't say out loud, mostly because they weren't for Sam's ears. I wouldn't tell Banner, either, how my love for him went even deeper after learning he hadn't rushed me, because in a few hours, none of that would matter. Yes, even after understanding Banner's role in Sam offering to marry me. I could be angry about it... but why waste the energy on something that happened years ago, when I wouldn't have been with him, even if I had told him the truth?

I didn't want that. He made me happy and as soon as I walked downstairs, we would get married. Become husband and wife, after years' worth of angst and heartache, something I was more than ready for.

Ready to face the future, to spend the rest of my life with him, to handle whatever came our way head on.

So, I held out my arm, smiled at Sam, and enjoyed the slow descent down the steps toward the gorgeous, loving man waiting for me at the bottom.

He was ready to move forward as I was. And finally, the moment we said our "I do's" became the one I would cherish forever, no matter what the future held for us.

"Banner?"

"Hmm?"

We were in bed, long after our small wedding ended, and our friends finished off the wine before leaving us all alone for the evening. Sam left with Sarah clinging to his arm, once she came to me asking if it was okay for her to like him. I told her the last thing I would ever tell someone was who they could take interest in.

Banner found the whole situation funny and perhaps, to someone else looking in, this whole thing would've looked ridiculous to them. I married a man who loved me, treated me well, and was able not only to support himself, but a family more than adequately.

Wasn't that something anybody would be happy to find in a lifelong partner?

I knew it was, yet here in bed next to him, suddenly I began to worry about the future. As if I hadn't had enough worries over the last few years to last me a lifetime.

I reached down between our bodies. Grabbing his hand, I dared to say my thoughts out loud, because there was no doubt he could handle it. "I'm scared. That this isn't real, that I'll wake up and you won't be next to me. That after all this... something... something is going to go wrong."

"Val." He moved quick, covering my body with his and

kissing me long, deep, and lovingly. By the time he freed my mouth, I had to take in a deep breath to steady myself as he said, "I know why you're afraid. But I promise you, I will do everything in my power to ensure we're never apart again. We're both here, this is real, and I'm not leaving, no matter what happens from this moment forward."

"You swear?"

It was childish, immature, and a crazy question after everything — the stuff I was responsible for putting us through — but he got it. He got me.

And, amazing man that he was, he lifted his hand with pinky out, laughing. "Pinky swear, sweetheart."

My pinky met his. They hooked together as we gazed into each other's eyes and smiled. Then he took his away so we could move on to sexier, more enjoyable activities that involved neither of us leaving the bed until morning.

Our wedding day had been perfect. For quite a while after that day, everything else was, too, until the one thing I wanted more than anything refused to happen.

And I began to believe it never would.

CHAPTER 21

AUGUST 4TH

ONE YEAR.

One wonderful, life-changing, beautiful year later where my world had flipped upside down... where the wonderful man I married told me he wanted to have a family with me. Yet here I sat in the bathroom, crying my eyes out as I started my period right on time.

I didn't understand. Didn't know why I wasn't getting pregnant when I was doing everything right. Doing all the things the doctor told me to do including timing sex perfectly.

What was wrong?

Why wasn't the thing I wanted most happening?

My entire life was better than the first time. I wasn't stressed, was married, and lived in a house with enough space for us to have two children or more, and yet...

Each month, my body failed to do the one thing I

wanted it do more than anything else, something I didn't understand no matter how hard I tried.

Banner tried to remain patient and understanding, but even he suggested we stop trying, to relax a little, to see what happened. He didn't think we were in a rush and okay, it wasn't like my biological clock was ticking.

Everyone kept mentioning how I wasn't even thirty yet, that I had plenty of time for children, but they didn't know what it was like for me. I had already been pregnant, with a child I ended up losing, and every month my period showed up had become a reminder of that.

I cried harder, more intensely than every month before now, until I couldn't cry anymore. Even though Banner wouldn't return for hours, I couldn't let him see me like this. When he came home, he would know, though. Somehow, that man could tell I had been crying even if hours had passed, and he would do his best to comfort me.

This time, though, there would be more options. Because a year without conceiving meant doctors and tests, to see if anything was wrong with either of us. To see if something was preventing this perfectly normal event from occurring.

After splashing water on my face and redoing the tiny bit of makeup I bothered to wear, I left the bathroom. I had to find something to do today that didn't involve wallowing in despair over this thing I couldn't control.

Grabbing the one glass of wine I would drink today

from the kitchen, I strode into the living room. Turning on the TV with the volume low, I pulled my phone out from my pocket.

Then, I called Sarah, figuring that her continuing love affair with Sam would amuse me for a little bit. When she answered the phone, I giggled at her breathless, "Um, hi, Val."

"Please don't tell me I'm interrupting something. Again."

It seemed every time I called, she and Sam were in bed. Not that I cared they couldn't get enough of each other. I knew what that felt like. The few times I'd spent time with them since our wedding, I figured it wouldn't be long before they were announcing their engagement. I honestly looked forward to that because they both deserved to have someone special in their lives.

"Um... no. No, of course not." I had to bite my lip when there was a distinct slapping sound and a squeak before she said, "I mean, can I call you back? Like, five minutes, Val. I promise."

"Sure. I'll give you six and a half, just to make sure you've really got time to talk."

She groaned, I busted out laughing, and hung up on the call before she could say anything else.

Seriously, they were like rabbits. Kind of like how Banner and I had been before we were actually advised to cool it a bit around ovulation time. Something about how having sex constantly might actually be bad when you're trying to get pregnant. To have sex at specific times and days and not much more, at least during that window of time.

Whatever. We continued to mostly do it whenever we wanted to.

At this point, I was ready to try anything, which I'm sure bothered Banner a bit since he would no doubt place money on most things not being the cause of our issues.

There I went again, mulling over not being able to get pregnant. Sighing, I gulped down the wine, put the glass on the side table, turned the TV up and grabbed a pillow to put under my head.

I fell sound asleep waiting for Sarah to call me back. It actually took her thirty minutes when I looked at my call log upon waking two hours later. To my surprise, there were two missed calls from mother, yet no message.

Needless to say, after the year of silence from her end, I decided what she had to say obviously wasn't that important and didn't bother to return her call.

Instead, I got up from the couch and went to freshen up before Banner came home.

Normal.

Unbelievable. Every single test the doctor could

perform, she did, and there wasn't any issue she could find that prevented us from me getting pregnant.

How could that be?

Normal.

Normal?

Normal.

Maybe if I kept repeating that word inside my head, I would believe what that word meant. Normal meant waiting for nature to take its course, for things to happen on their own and in their own time.

No choice.

That's what it gave Banner and I. We had no choice except to let things happen because we had many years ahead of us to try again. To have fun, not stress over it, and no matter how sad I became when it didn't happen that month, to remember I had the privilege of trying again.

Well, I needed to, since the way I'd been handling things wasn't great and needed to stop crying over the situation.

So, as Banner held my hand as he drove us home from the doctor's office, I gave his hand a squeeze, and smiled when he glanced over at me.

"You doing okay?"

"Yes." Taking a deep breath, I let it out slowly and nodded. "Thank you for being patient with me. This has been rough on me but I'm just so happy to know for sure that we just have to keep trying."

He kissed the back of my hand. "And I want to keep trying, Val."

It was something in the tone of his voice that made me ask, "But...?"

"There isn't one."

"Really? Because I get the feeling you want to say something else."

Sighing, he placed my hand back on my lap and his expression went from tender to concerned. "I wanted to suggest we take a break."

"That isn't trying, though."

"No, it isn't, but maybe when you talk to your mother, you'll know why I'm saying this."

Stunned, the only words I could manage to get out of my mouth were, "What? You talked to my mother?"

"Of course not, Val. I spoke with mine, as you're well aware she's continued despite pressure from your mother. She told me your mother has called you several times over the past few weeks. Why didn't you tell me?"

"Why? How about I haven't answered the phone? I don't know why she's calling me. She hasn't left a message and the last thing I want to do is listen to her lecture me just because—"

"Val." Banner cut me off gently, his expression softening, and my stomach sank to the floor as he explained. "She's not calling to lecture you, sweetheart. It's your father. He's sick."

The tears I wanted so hard to get rid of returned with a vengeance. My heart clenched as if someone had just squeezed it with a vise, and I was glad to already be sitting down.

"Oh, my god."

She hadn't left an answer because that's not the sort of news you break to anyone over a voicemail. I should have answered the phone. I was a terrible daughter for not picking up the phone the first time. For letting my anger get in the way of my mother trying to reach out to me, whatever the reason.

I didn't ask Banner for any other details. Taking my cell out, I finally returned my mother's calls.

Early the next morning, we were on a flight back to Ohio, all while I prayed we wouldn't arrive too late for me to beg my father's forgiveness.

CHAPTER 22

AUGUST 5TH

"You can't come in."

My mother stood on the other side of the door, cracked so she could speak to us without enough room for us to come inside. My heart broke upon realizing what she was doing, how she used this moment to get what she wanted even briefly.

"Mom—"

"No. He needs to leave or I won't let you in."

Banner squeeze my hand. "It's all right, Val."

"It isn't." Tears slid down my cheeks, my back straightening in defiance and in hurt. How could she do this after begging me to come home to see my dad? "Mom, he's my husband. I want him here."

"And I don't. You want to see your father, you'll do it without him."

What could I do? Banner wouldn't make me choose.

He would walk away, let me see my father, because that's who he was. We both knew why she acted this way. Nothing we said in that moment — just like all the times before — would change her mind.

And I couldn't use this moment to stand my ground. Not when my father was on the other side of that door, waiting to see his only daughter as he laid struggling with each breath.

"I can't believe you," I said to her through gritted teeth, both my hands clenched into fists as Banner let go and stepped back. "How could you hurt me like this right now? When I need him?"

She didn't answer, merely stared at me with her red, swollen eyes, refusing to open the door even an inch more until Banner left. I turned to him, trying to swallow my anger and hold onto my dignity in a moment where I felt like I had none, all so I wouldn't miss saying goodbye to my father.

He pulled me into his arms, kissed the top of my head, and said, "I'll call you later, sweetheart."

Then, since he was the kindest, sweetest man I had ever known next to my father, he said to my mother, "I'm sorry, Aunt Rose," before turning and walking away, leaving me alone for what would be one of the hardest moments in my life.

And I know he had no choice. He wouldn't let me choose staying with him over seeing my father, even if I wanted to... and I didn't. I loved my father; there wasn't any way I wasn't going to stay by his side until he took his last breath.

So, I lifted my bag as my mother opened the door to let me inside, and without a word, I stalked past her to my old room, where I tossed the luggage before heading to my parent's bedroom to hold my father's hand.

THE MAN LYING IN THE BED BARELY RESEMBLED THE vibrant, cheerful man I last saw a year ago.

No way to stop the tears or the way it felt like my heart was being ripped out of my chest. I took his hand in mine, and he didn't even open his eyes when I softly said, "Dad, I'm here."

I sat down in the chair beside the bed, crying hard enough my shoulders shook, listening to his harsh breathing. Why hadn't my mother called me a lot sooner. Surely, he hadn't gotten this sick within the last three weeks?

And even if he had, why hadn't my brothers tried to call me? Why would Judy wait until my mother couldn't get ahold of me for weeks before she told Banner what was going on?

I didn't deserve that. No matter what I had done, loving Banner and marrying him had nothing to do with my relationship with my father. I had deserved to know the truth as soon as possible. She could have left a message saying it was urgent; I would've responded to that.

As my anger grew, my tears intensified, until they came so hard and fast I couldn't see anything. I lowered my head to the bed, holding my father's hand tight with both of mine, and kissed the back of his hand, begging the world to at least give me the chance to talk to him one more time.

Time passed slowly as I sat there, waiting for my father to open his eyes and tell me this was all a bad dream, but three hours after my arrival, he hadn't even moved a finger.

Although leaving him was the last thing I wanted to do, the entire trip and my mother's behavior had exhausted me, and I needed to take a small nap. Standing up, I bent over and kissed him on the cheek, whispered, "I love you, Dad," and quietly left the room.

My mother stood in the hallway, back against the wall and arms crossed over her chest. Her head shot up at the click of the bedroom door and when she opened her mouth to speak, I lifted a hand to stop anything she wanted to say.

"Don't. Right now, the best thing we can both do is say nothing at all."

"Val—"

"I said don't!" When I tried to get past her, she grabbed my arm and because I didn't want to hurt her by yanking myself free, I stopped walking and glared at her. "Let me go."

"I don't want to fight." Her statement was soft, her cheeks wet from crying. "I'm just glad you're home."

"I'm not here for you, Mom." Tugging my arm free, I retreated a step and shook my head, engaging in a battle I wished to avoid yet couldn't. "How could you wait this long to tell me? He's my father and the last time I saw him... how could you?"

Now her tone was defensive, her arms crossed again. "I called you."

"Really? You called?" I pointed at her bedroom door, hissing, "He's been sick for more than a month, Mom. You don't get that way overnight!"

"The cancer..." Her lower lip wobbled, tears leaking from her eyes again. "It progressed quickly, Valerie. By the time the doctor's diagnosed him, there wasn't anything they could do."

"So, you leave me a message!" The words came out angry, shouted, and my whole body shook. My mother's eyes widened because never in my entire life had I ever raised my voice at her. "You could have said enough to let me know it was urgent. Anything except calling for weeks on end and leaving it at that."

"And you could have answered the phone instead of ignoring my calls. Don't blame your childishness in this matter on me."

"Wow." The word was a whisper, filled with disbelief and distaste for the woman who gave me an ultimatum, then blamed the result on me. "I can't believe you're putting this on me, after the way you behaved, both then and earlier today. Why would I answer the phone when you've been so cruel to me? To Banner?"

She didn't respond to that, rubbing her hands together, and staring at my face. Her mouth was slightly open, as if she wanted to say something, but couldn't get the words to come forth.

Then, her shoulders drooped as she repeated her earlier statement. "I don't want to fight."

Neither did I. There wasn't anything either of us could say that would change the past, that would make up for the time missed.

Exhausted, I simply responded, "I'm going to lay down for a little. Please come get me if he wakes up."

At her nod, I headed to my old room, and cried myself to sleep.

"I LOVED HIM."

The statement from my mother came out of nowhere later that evening after we ate dinner and I stood at the sink, washing dishes.

I made dinner after sitting again with my father for hours, hoping he would wake up, yet having to come to terms with the fact that probably wouldn't happen since he was only receiving comfort care.

We might have only hours, or days, until he passed away. Mom told me my brothers had already been here to say goodbye to Dad, but neither could stay since they couldn't miss work.

I understood, truly. Both my brothers and their wives worked full-time, whereas I didn't need to because of Banner. That's why I would be here until the end, unlike them, which made me sad for them and my mother.

Again, couldn't change the past or even how things were now, so instead, I focused on what my mother said, her words confusing me. "What? You loved who?"

"Banner's father. I loved him."

My hands, in the middle of rinsing off a plate, went motionless. After a moment where neither of us said anything, I finished rinsing and put it in the strainer. Shutting off the water, I turned around and leaned against the counter, barely managing to croak out, "What?"

"Judy stole him." My mother sat at the table, staring down at the table and continuing to talk, as if she didn't dare look at me while telling me this. "We were best friends and she knew how I felt about him. She didn't care. She wanted him. Ran off with him and got married."

"Mom..."

She continued on without hearing me. "I loved him. He

was my first. Your father never knew that, you know. That we slept together, that is. We were both seniors in high school and neither of us ever dated anyone else, but we were curious."

Holy shit. "Okay, okay. Stop."

Finally lifting her head, she laughed, but it wasn't a happy one. "My problem with you and this relationship goes far beyond you two being cousins, Valerie. You're married to the son of the only other man I've ever loved besides your father and now, I can't bear to look at him."

What in the hell was I supposed to say to that? "I don't understand why you're telling me this."

"I didn't raise you to act this way," she muttered, her gaze dropping again. "To disregard the feelings of others, especially among your family. To lie and cover up the truth from us. Where is your shame?"

"I was ashamed, Mom. You think I wanted all that to happen? You don't think I fought against my feelings for him, that I didn't find it as wrong as you did at first?" My eyes burned, yet no tears; they had finally run out. "I fought against it, for you and for dad. Fought against how deep my feelings were for years. We slept together once and if it weren't for... for the pregnancy..."

She looked at me then, eyes glistening in the low light, and waited for me to continue.

"Things probably would have been different if it weren't for that." That wasn't completely true. I had little doubt Banner and I would have ended up together no matter how much we fought the attraction. However, that was one thing she didn't need to hear. "But you don't get to tell me I ignored your feelings. Because for too long, they were all I thought about, instead of appreciating how much Banner loves me. You loved his father and the fact he chose Judy, married Judy, isn't his fault or mine. And if you can't or won't accept the fact we love each other, that we're married, then that's on you from this moment forward."

If she wanted to reply, she never got the chance as a wailing cry rang through the house and we both took off running toward the bedroom.

CHAPTER 23

AUGUST 10TH

My father died in my arms minutes after we entered the room that night. My mother held his hand as I hugged his upper body, crying into his neck as I told him over and over how much I loved him.

The days since have dragged by, my mother in a haze nobody seemed able to penetrate, which left me to handle the final arrangements.

And now, here we were at the cemetery, the rain pouring down on us while watching my father's coffin being slowly lowered into the waiting ground.

Judy and my mother stood next to one another, weeping into each other's arms, with me and Banner to their left, my brothers and their wives on the right.

Even though I had been there when it happened, I couldn't believe my father was gone. That the only way I would ever see his face or hear his voice again would be through old photos and videos. Never again would he hug me, tell me how much he loved me, or verbalize how proud he was.

Worse, I was angry. At my mother and myself. No matter her reaction, I should've pushed back, not let her get away with shoving me out of their lives unless I did what she wanted. That was my fault, my failing, because maybe if I had been around, I would've noticed my father getting sick and gotten him help sooner.

What if. Maybe. Perhaps.

I knew all of that kind of wishing and thinking was pointless. There wasn't anything I could do now. Being angry didn't even make sense when nothing could be done, yet I knew this feeling wouldn't go away any time soon.

"Val?" Banner murmured the words into my ear, his arm tightening around my waist. "Everyone's left."

Jerking my head up from where I stared at the ground to discover we were the only two people remaining at my father's grave, I leaned into Banner's hold and sighed. "I don't know what to do."

"About your mother?"

"Yeah." There hadn't been any reason to keep what my mother told me from him, so now he knew and had been as dumbfounded by her admission as I was. "She'll never accept us, but she's my mother. I...I... I don't want this to happen again. I don't want to be attending my mother's funeral after not speaking with her. What am I supposed to do?"

"Tell her."

A simple answer for a simple solution, only it wasn't.

"I tried."

"Try again, sweetheart. Make her listen." He kissed the top of my head. "All you can do is try."

"I know. And my brothers...god, they wouldn't even speak to me at our father's funeral! It's ridiculous."

"Yes, it is." Clearing his throat, probably to keep from saying something that might not be too nice yet totally deserving about my brothers' behavior, he grabbed my hand and took a step back. "How about leaving it until tomorrow? Let's go back to the apartment, relax, and get some rest. Then, try talking to your mother again tomorrow."

Sounded like a good idea. I would think about what to say later, too tired in this moment to fight with her anymore. "Okay."

Exhausted, I held his hand tight as he led the way back to the car. We didn't even make it onto the main road before I fell into the deepest slumber I'd experienced since arriving back home.

This time, I showed up to my mother's house on

my own, alone, and let myself in after my knock went unanswered, the doorbell ignored.

"Mom?"

It wasn't a question of her presence. I knew she was home. Her car was in the driveway, as was Judy's. Neither of them responded, though, so I shut the door behind me and strode down the hallway toward the kitchen.

They were sitting at the table, looking through a photo album, and laughing softly. I stopped in the doorway, watching as my mother pointed at another photo that led them both to laughing louder, then covering their mouth as if their own amusement shocked them both.

That's when my mother spotted me, her hands dropping as her expression changed, all merriment fleeing as she frowned.

Not really the kind of welcome I wanted from the only parent I had left as I pointed at the table and said, "Hi. Which album is that?"

Judy sniffled, answering, "Mine. I was sharing some photos from after we moved to London," as she closed the album sharply.

I got the hint. Those pictures weren't going to get shared with me. I tried not to care, especially since I came to tell my mother her issues weren't mine and to get over herself. I could already tell it wouldn't go well.

Didn't help when she rose from her seat, crossing her arms as she said, "I thought you two left after the funeral."

"Is that what you want?" Barely holding back the tears, I swallowed my hurt. "For me to leave?"

"You don't care about what I want, Valerie. You've made that quite clear."

"That isn't true. Would I be here if that was true?"

My aunt sighed, the sound long and drawn out as she answered the question. "You feel guilty, my dear, as you should. If you had done as we asked, you would've been here for your father's illness."

I hated the cruelty. Yes, that was true. If I hadn't stayed at Banner's place — if I had returned home the day they both showed up there — we wouldn't have moved away or married each other. I might have continued living at home with my parents and known the exact moment my father became sick.

Unavoidable truth, all of it.

I accepted those facts. I had to. That time I missed with my father? Gone forever. I would never get that back.

Why couldn't my mother and Judy accept what was right in front of them? And why did they expect me to change when they hadn't? Wouldn't?

"Mom?"

She faced me, having turned away to look out the kitchen window, and stared at me, her face blank. "Hmm?"

"You're clinging to the past, to what was, and you're blaming me for it. Things changed. You're the one not accepting things as they are now." I swiped at an escaped tear as she huffed, her face coloring with heat, afraid her secret love would be revealed to Judy. I wouldn't sink to her level, though. "I care about what you want and understand why you think the way you do. Have you even tried to see things from my point of view? Tried to understand why I love him, the son of your best friend?"

"I..." She blinked and shook her head. "It doesn't matter."

"Wrong. It does matter. It may not mean anything to you and that's fine, but our love is real. Meaningful. We care about each other. Nothing you say, nothing you do, will make me love you any less or... or shove you out of my life because of the way you're treating me over this."

"That's enough, my dear." Judy stood, putting her around my mother's shoulders as if it would protect her from my words and frowned at me. "You've said your piece. I think you should go now."

My mother's gaze wouldn't meet my own, flicking away when I looked to see her thoughts on the suggestion, which told me all I needed to know.

But, I knew her. She would think about what I said, mull the words over and over in her mind, until she either agreed with me or not. I wouldn't win her over by insisting on staying and talking more.

For now, I had done all I could. Nodding, I stepped back and before turning on my heel to go, smiled at my mother, saying, "I love you."

Then, I left and headed to the casino, ready to return home with Banner. To go back to the life we had built with each other, hoping everything would fall into place sooner rather than later.

Unfortunately, for the both of us, some things never changed.

CHAPTER 24
MAY 31ST

People were stubborn.

Take me, for example.

I always considered the trait something I received from my father. He never gave up. As a child and a young adult, I always admired that about him and never considered the fact my mother was stubborn at all.

In fact, she seemed to melt around him, but there was no doubt now... my mother never showed how single-minded and inflexible she was in front of us kids. If I could bet on it, and know for certain, I would wager decisions were made in private — my mother being the one in control — and my father merely followed through with them.

I knew this now, because months had passed and my mother hadn't called, not once. Me? I called her, every single day, and she hadn't picked up the phone or returned any of my calls.

At first, I cried over it, because I really didn't want us to become estranged. I didn't want her funeral to be the next and final time we were in the same place.

However, what could I do? I couldn't make her talk to me or see me. Other than going home to force my way into us being in the same room together... what else was there?

No part of me wanted to let her go, allow her to shove me out of her life. But if that's what she wanted, did I really have the right to insist otherwise when I didn't like how she demanded I end things with Banner?

So, I stopped crying, and as of yesterday, I stopped calling her, too. She had Judy, which meant she wasn't alone, and that brought me a little comfort, at least.

It was why, even though we were back in Cleveland, we drove past the house yesterday without stopping by. I refused to let the whole situation get me down any longer.

After all, Sam and Sarah were getting married today, a happy occasion that required me to push my troubles aside to celebrate with my friends.

In this little room inside the church, both Macy and I teared up at how beautiful Sarah looked in her dress as she stood in front of the mirror. The fact she couldn't stop smiling, however, was the best of all, and reminded me of when I finally married Banner.

To know they felt that kind of love for each other?

Lucky them. And although I had loved Sam, he had been correct. My feelings would never have risen to the same level as the ones I had for Banner, leaving me quite thrilled Sam was marrying someone whose did. Even better that the woman was one of my best friends and I knew they would treat each other well.

"Ten minutes." Macy adjusted Sarah's veil. "Anything else you need?"

"Nope." She smoothed her dress, took a deep breath, and then turned to face us with a nervous smile. "Actually, um, yes."

"What?" She looked in my direction at the question, Macy followed, and my stomach flipped. "Is it bad?"

"No!" Laughing, she lifted her train and walked over to me. "Everything is great. I just..." She flashed me a smile, her cheeks coloring as she placed both hands flat on her stomach. "I'm pregnant."

Oh. Her nervousness made sense now. How long had she put off telling me because of what happened with my first pregnancy? I loved her for caring.

"Sarah..." Taking her hands in mine, I gave them a squeeze, tears gathering in my eyes. "I'm so happy for you."

"Then why do you look like you're about to cry?"

"Because you're sweet, to worry about telling me, but you shouldn't have. Yes, thinking about my daughter makes me sad and no, I don't really talk about her or what happened. Doesn't mean I want you to avoid telling me something like this!"

"Okay." She tugged her hands free and pulled me into a hug. "Well, then I guess you should know I'm fourteen weeks and no, this isn't a shotgun wedding."

"Of course not. We would all kick Sam's ass if that were the case."

Sarah drew back, laughing when Macy took a turn embracing her, before fanning her face as she asked, "My makeup didn't run, right?"

"Nope, it's perfect."

"Good." After indulging in one final examination of her hair and dress in the mirror, Sarah looped her arm through Macy's with a smile. "After this, we need to help this girl here find someone so she can get married, too."

"Oh geez." Macy rolled her eyes. "I don't need help finding a man. I don't even know if I want to get married."

Sarah mimicked the action. "Please. You were trying on wedding dresses, too! Don't deny it."

Macy bent her arm, like she was going to elbow Sarah in the side. Her opportunity was taken away by the arrival of Sarah's dad who announced the time had come to walk down the aisle.

The ceremony itself was lovely.

Mostly, I enjoyed watching their expressions as they exchanged vows, while I sat next to Banner. He held my hand tight. Although we both managed to keep our eyes on our friends as they exchanged vows, there were occasional side glances.

Those looks overflowed with shared remembrances of our own wedding.

When they kissed, Banner bent his head close to kiss my cheek, lingering until I turned my head and met his lips with mine. He drew away, his smile bright as his attention returned to our friends.

Mine didn't. I kept my eyes on him.

I loved this man. Didn't know what I would do without him. And I didn't have to imagine my life without him in it; I already knew what that was like. Definitely never wanted to experience that again.

But my mother? My brothers? I missed them. They were my family and refused to speak to me. Although the four-year difference between us often meant my brothers and I never did much together outside of family activities, I still loved and wanted them to be part of my life. However, they were also twins, which meant they'd always had and continued to rely each other, while I had ended up being closer to our parents.

A tear escaped one eye as I sat here thinking about the whole situation. Banner, no doubt associating the swiping of the tear off my cheek as emotion about the ceremony, gave my hand a squeeze as Sarah and Sam strolled down the aisle, hand-in-hand now as a married couple.

I smiled at him, and them, through my sadness. All the

thoughts in my head came around to me loving Banner, to not wanting to hurt him, and to knowing my life would always have something missing because no matter what decision I made, somebody wouldn't be happy about it.

And I chose him, again. Through everything, over the years, I always came back to him. That would never change, so the fighting was over. No more arguing with myself about what the right thing to do was and whether or not I would regret it later.

Not possible.

I would never regret loving him. He was my husband, my best friend, and the love of my life. We'd spend the rest of our lives together, hopefully with children of our own.

Something we wanted more than anything else and, despite my attempts to hope otherwise, the one thing I slowly began to believe we were never meant to have.

CHAPTER 25

DECEMBER 1ST

SARAH'S SON, BORN ONLY A FEW HOURS AGO, LAID ON my chest in her room at the hospital.

There had been no way I would turn down her request to come visit her and the baby, especially at the hesitation in her voice when she asked. I understood — and loved — how much she cared about my feelings... which is exactly why I didn't say no, even though my heart twinged in pain the instant I held her little boy in my arms.

The pangs were resentment, which made me feel awful because that was the last thing I wanted to feel toward my best friend's kid, who was a perfect mix of Sarah and Sam rolled into one.

At that thought, tears pricked my eyes, because my little girl's face came to mind. It wasn't that I didn't want to think about her; truly, she was never far from my mind.

She would've been turning three in just a couple

weeks. That's all I could think about and I had to hide my face to shield the tears creeping down my cheeks, nuzzling the top of the baby's head.

So far, I had managed to hide my pain. Not even Banner knew that the closer the days until to her birthday, the harder it became to pretend I wasn't upset at the fact another pregnancy hadn't happened yet.

My thoughts had turned into an obsession, one I thought about all the time even when I didn't want to, tried hard not to. And yes, sometimes I hated how much having another child with Banner mattered to me.

Enough I held Sarah's little boy as long as I could, which ended up being over an hour since both she and Sam fell asleep. By the time they woke up, the baby was hungry and I was more than ready to leave.

Handing him over into his mother's waiting arms, I whispered my congratulations once more, then left to return home, where I would wallow in my self-pity until Banner came home to distract me from the pain.

"You doing okay, Val?"

The question distracted me from the incredibly cute kitten video on my phone. I looked up to see Banner leaning against the door frame, hands in his pockets and eyes filled with concern.

I didn't have to answer him. Here it was, nearly seven o'clock and I hadn't even noticed him coming home or standing in the doorway. Too busy trying to keep myself distracted from the feelings coursing through me all day long.

At the shake of my head, he walked over to the couch and sat down beside me, pulling me into his side. I rested my head on his shoulder, both of us sitting in silence because there wasn't one thing he could say to me. Nothing would make me feel better and I loved him for knowing that, for understanding they were my emotions to deal with. That all he could do was comfort me and be there for me to listen if I wanted to talk about it, which I didn't, because we had already talked about this so many times.

Thirty minutes or so passed before he sighed, kissed the top of my head, and spoke softly. "Maybe having something to do might help. I don't believe being home all day is good for you because it gives you too much time to think."

"I know." Couldn't disagree with him there. "It's not thinking, it's obsessing, and I know it's not good for me. All those months of therapy did teach me something."

Moving away from him as he chuckled, I sat up and shoved my hair out of my eyes, sighing. "What do you think I should do?"

"That's something you need to figure out, Val. You

should know what you can do to fill your time." He put his hand over mine and smiled. "Not that I don't care but do you really want me to tell you what to do?"

I shrugged. "Dunno. What are you suggesting? I don't need to work, you even told me that."

"I did. No matter what you do, I have things taken care of Val. That doesn't mean you can't work if you want to, find a job you actually want to do instead of one you have to do. There's also volunteering. Whatever you want to do, I'm here for you."

"Of course, you are. I haven't thought about work, but you're right. I did like my job before and I'm so sick of feeling this way. The disappointment is hard to deal with and maybe it won't be so bad if I have something else to focus on. Right?"

He gazed at me, smiling and not saying a word, because of course that's what he thought. I needed something else in my life, another thing to focus on, and I knew he was right.

How long had he been thinking about this, waiting for the right moment to bring it up? I guess it didn't matter, not really, because we both knew this whole situation had been going on for way too long now.

"I'll look into it." I smiled and then rolled my eyes at realizing something. "We'll see if anyone will even hire me considering it's been how long since I had a job?"

"Don't be ridiculous." He hauled me into his lap, slid

his hand around the back of my head, and pulled me down for a long, lingering kiss. "Nobody will be careless enough to pass up someone with your resume."

"Sure, sure."

Much as I blew his comment off, we both knew I appreciated his faith in me, and the fact he was correct, too. I worked hard in school and after, before everything happened between us. Many things in my life could be — and have been — questioned, but my work ethic had never been one of them.

And the more I thought about it as the days passed, the more I knew that going back to work was exactly what I needed to do.

But for the rest of that evening, I spent all my energy on showing Banner just how much I loved him and secretly continued hoping for a child that would complete our family.

CHAPTER 26

DECEMBER 22ND

Damn, exhaustion didn't even begin to define how tired I was.

As I entered the house, a hallway light turned on automatically, but it wouldn't be long before it shut off. It was weird, coming home to all the lights off, especially since Banner's car was in the garage.

Not that I called out for him with the size of the house, since he probably wouldn't hear me anyway.

Maybe he was in his office, which was upstairs in the back of the house, so I wouldn't see the light on from outside. He spent more time at home lately. He joked it was the only way he could see me because of the ever changing odd and late hours I'd been keeping with my job.

Turned out, when I returned to work, I remembered how much enjoyment my career brought to me, and quickly went from part-time to full-time.

And it had helped in keeping me distracted from the fact I wasn't getting pregnant. At first, I thought about it, of course, but now a year had passed since I began working again and the fact didn't bug me like before.

Sure, I was a little disappointed every time my period showed up. It was difficult not to be because it was such an unavoidable reminder from my own body, yet the sting had gone away slowly. I didn't cry anymore. I shrugged and got on with my day, letting Banner know, and he was great about it, too.

"More time with just us." He would say that before pulling me into his arms and kissing me until we were both thinking about what it would lead to later. "More time for us to do this without interruption."

For the most part, that's how it was constantly now: just us. We saw Sarah and Sam on occasion. They would typically come down for a weekend here and there, along with their son, who was one now. It led to me thinking about my little girl more often than before, which was okay, because the hurt was more like a chest squeeze now instead of the stabbing pains I used to get.

And Macy, she didn't visit that often, but we kept in touch, although a little less than before. She moved across the ocean for a job in Germany and was having the time of her life. She occasionally videoed when we both had a free moment, the most recent being earlier today where she told me an amazing man she thought might be the one for her had asked her out on their first date.

I told her if she chose to live across the ocean permanently, I'd have to kick her ass, and she laughed before blowing me a kiss and ending the call with a wink.

So yep, it was mostly me and Banner because I really hadn't managed to make any new friends, which didn't bother me. I think Banner thought I would make some when I started working. Turned out, it was more difficult to make new friends as an adult. Sure, we had lunches and stuff, but mostly, I just wanted to spend any free time I had at home with Banner.

And thinking of him...

Slipping off my heels, I headed up the steps and toward his office, only to see the light was off in there as well.

Odd.

It was only ten o'clock. Was he already asleep? If so, that's the earlier he'd ever gone to bed and I walked faster toward our bedroom. Was he sick? If he was, why didn't he call me?

And that's exactly where he was — sound asleep under the blankets, the window open to let in cooler air from outside.

No medicine sitting next to the bed, though, so maybe he was just tired.

I leaned over, kissed his cheek, and turned around to

leave when he grabbed my hand, groaning.

"Val... what time is it?" His question, whispered, sounded weak, and nothing like Banner at all.

"Just after ten." I could barely make him out in the darkness of the room, only enough to see the shadow of his other arm lifting off the bed to rub his face. "I'm sorry, I didn't mean to wake you up."

"Don't be." He sat up slowly and moved his head side to side, then sighed. "Good, it's gone."

"What?"

"Migraine. Came on fast this time."

"Another one?" With a heavy sigh of my own, I sat on the edge of the bed and squeezed his hand. "Maybe it's time to see a doctor about this. They've been going on for weeks now."

"Barely." He chuckled and kissed my cheek. "Don't worry, all right? If I feel like I need to go to the doctor, I will, but they aren't all that often. Maybe I'm overdoing it somehow."

"If anyone here is working too much, that would be me, don't you think?"

"I'm down for anything that makes you happy, sweetheart." Clearing his throat, he tossed the blankets aside and tugged me closer, hand cupping my cheek as he kissed me long and sweet. "Let me get a shower, then we'll eat something? I'm starving."

"All right. Something light, though, because I'm

beyond ready for bed."

When I stood up, he slid out of bed and wrapped me in his arms, kissing me again before whispering, "Ten minutes," and walking toward the bathroom.

As he did that, I took my phone from my pocket and typed in a reminder to make him call the doctor for an appointment; he would do it if I kept on him about seeing someone.

Then I headed downstairs to find something for us to eat.

"SEE? I'M FINE." THE DOCTOR HAD JUST LEFT THE room and Banner slipped back into his shirt while shaking his head at me. "I hope you feel better now. I hate when you worry."

"Why would I feel better? He said your blood pressure is a little high."

"Val. I'll do what he recommended, okay? Take the medication. Reduce my stress. Cut back on caffeine and red meat." He practically growled the last one, then winked at me. "Bastard."

"This isn't funny, Banner." I swallowed hard, my stomach twisting into knots. "Your father died of a heart attack!"

"Sorry, sweetheart." The amusement in his face

disappeared as he pulled me into his arms and rested his chin on the top of my head. "I hear you and the doctor. You heard what he said, though. I'm young and otherwise healthy. If you're stressing, it will stress me, so let's just try to take it easy, all right?"

"Yeah."

I tried to mean it, to do as he asked. We left the doctor's office and while he drove, I looked up some new recipes to try out. Both of us would have to eat better, so this would help us figure out what to pick up at the grocery store on the way home.

But like anyone with a tendency to become obsessed with something, along with way too much information available on the internet, there wasn't any chance I would avoid worrying over the potential outcomes from having high blood pressure.

Not that I let Banner have any idea of how much the horrible things that could happen to him ran through my mind on a constant loop.

Focusing at work became harder since I spent my time wondering if I would go home to find him in bed again with a terrible migraine that made it difficult for him to function.

Even as he ate better and tried to sleep the recommended seven hours minimum, both things I did with him so we could both be at our healthiest, it wasn't enough. No migraines after a week? Two? Didn't matter.

The thought that any moment they could come back terrified me.

On the particularly bad days when the thoughts took over everything, like tonight, I watched him sleep because I couldn't rest and wanted to do nothing else except remain close to him.

What would I do without him?

I had my friends, but otherwise, what did I have?

Perhaps it was crazy. I had a great job that I excelled at, where they already wanted to promote me to a manager position, and not only that, but I loved my work.

What was wrong with me?

I knew it wasn't right to feel that I would die without him, yet that's exactly what ran through my mind every time I thought about him no longer being alive. I didn't believe his eventual death would be something I survived even with the support of my friends, even if they were around for as long as I needed them to be despite having their own lives.

Banner had long ago become my life. I couldn't deny that fact any longer because no matter the fact we were together, there was a very real and undeniable fear inside me that he would leave me, someday, somehow, even if swore he wouldn't.

And with each day that passed, my feelings became harder to manage, to keep under control so Banner wouldn't have to worry about me on top of everything else.

CHAPTER 27
FEBRUARY 8TH

I PULLED INTO A SPOT IN THE PARKING LOT OF MY OB-GYN and shut off the engine.

Taking a deep breath, I opened the door and reached across the center console to grab my purse, then locked the car before climbing out.

Each visit to this office had become harder over the years. My annual exam results were the only good news that ever seemed to come from the place, but I hoped this time would be different.

My period was two weeks late and even though three separate pregnancy tests were negative, I didn't believe them. I knew my body, as well as how I felt the last time early on, and something was going on.

Good, bad, I didn't know, but I knew better than to ignore my health, especially after the way I nagged Banner to take care of himself.

After calling in early this morning, my doctor suggested coming in for a blood test just to make certain, and whatever the results, we would go from there. If I wasn't pregnant, then maybe my period was just late from stress or something...but one step at a time.

Letting out my breath, I headed inside and hoped with every bit of my heart that I would finally be pregnant again, just in time to surprise Banner for Valentine's Day if not our anniversary.

◈

AFTER THE NURSE DREW MY BLOOD, THE DOCTOR came in to talk about what would happen if the blood tests came back negative.

Then she said they would call me in a few days to let me know the results either way.

Even though she was super nice, I left the office feeling down, unable to relax because now I had to wait to find out the results. Waiting meant I couldn't tell Banner yet, mostly to avoid getting his hopes up, but remained unsure how he wouldn't figure it out since hiding my emotions from Banner never worked.

In the end, that didn't matter.

When he came home from the office, I was in the middle of cooking dinner. The way he touched my arm before leaning down to kiss my cheek seemed a little different than usual.

It wasn't an observation I could pinpoint down to anything specific, even as I turned around and wrapped my arms around neck, softly saying, "Hey there."

"Hi, sweetheart."

He sounded tired, more than he had in weeks, and I frowned upon meeting his red eyes. "Are you okay?"

"Yes." Sighing when I raised a brow to disagree, he shrugged and stepped back after dropping another kiss... on my forehead this time. "This day has been a little draining, that's all."

"Anything you want to talk about?"

"Not that I don't want to talk about it, sweetheart." His laugh wasn't a happy one as he rubbed the back of his neck. "More that I wouldn't even know where to begin. It's just been one of those days."

"Ah." I understood that and if he decided to tell me later, I would happily listen. "Well, dinner will be ready in about an hour. I've been a little behind today."

"No big deal." Running a hand through his hair, he blew out a breath and turned toward the fridge, opening it to grab a water. "Speaking of running, I should get mine in really quick, then grab a shower before dinner. We'll have a nice night in."

"I'd like that." When he turned to head upstairs, I called out, "Are you sure you want to go running? Why not just skip one, get a shower, and relax after the day you've had?"

"I'm on a roll, sweetheart. Can't stop now."

"Okay."

Maybe he heard something in that word or in my voice. He whirled around, walked back into the kitchen, and backed me up against the sink, a definite twinkle shining in his eyes. "Is there something you want to share with me, Val?"

Caught off guard, I stumbled. "N-no. Why would you think that?"

"Because I know everything." He chuckled, lowered his lips toward mine, and kissed me. It was soft, sweet... loving.

Everything he had always been and always would be.

When he drew away, I sighed and grabbed the collar of his shirt, growling with frustration. He couldn't know, not really considering not even I knew yet. And I wanted to tell him what might be happening, but I couldn't. Hopefully soon.

Instead, I distracted him with a pout, my eyes on his lips. "One kiss is never enough. How about another one before you take that run?"

He grinned. "Just one last kiss, huh? You know you stole that line from me."

"Yeah, yeah." Lifting a hand to his face, I cupped his cheek. My heart beat faster as he leaned into the touch, closing his eyes on a contented sigh that had me whispering, "Love you."

"I love you, too."

He turned his face, kissed my palm, then swooped in to give me the kiss I asked for. It was so much more than that, however. Lifting me in his arms, he spun us around and sat me on the table, his hands finding their way beneath my shirt as our tongues mingled.

I forgot about dinner. About his run. About whether or not I was pregnant.

About how tired he was.

All I could focus on was his touch, the way he ran his hands down the side of my body, before resting a single hand on my stomach.

Did he know?

I had no idea how, but maybe he did.

Or maybe, like me, he was merely hopeful of what might be.

When he ended the kiss, he winked and helped me down off the table before grabbing his water again and walking out of the kitchen, whistling.

Not that I was disappointed.

If anything, my whole body tingled with anticipation. I could barely wait for later because Banner had a habit of picking up right where he left off, which meant my evening would be an amazing one.

And as I went back to ensuring dinner would be ready

in an hour as promised, I found myself humming for the first time in what felt like years.

I should have known better.

Things going well hadn't ever been a strong theme in my life and for all those moments in the kitchen felt perfect, I shouldn't have ignored my instincts.

Standing on the porch, my foot tapped anxiously against the wood as I glanced down at my watch, over and over again.

Banner wasn't anywhere in sight. That wouldn't be so bad, except I knew his running route and he should returned from his run and came up the driveway ten minutes ago.

At first, I tried not to worry too much. He hated that and like he said, the more I worried about him, the more he did the same for me. It wasn't healthy for either us, but I also relied on the routine. I liked knowing how long his runs were and exactly what route he took, because then I knew when he would return.

Okay. Maybe he was stopped by a neighbor or someone he knew, but why not text? Was his phone dead? Did he forget to charge it?

In the interest of trying not to let him know I was

worrying, I hadn't sent him a text message yet, but now I couldn't wait any longer.

"Where are you?"

I typed the words, yet didn't send them. Too strong. Instead, I deleted them and went for something a little less worry-ish sounding. *"Dinner's almost ready. Get your butt back here!"*

Sending it, I breathed out at the whoosh sound and waited for his response, releasing my lip after it hurt to the point I realized my teeth were biting into the soft flesh.

That's when I heard the soft ping of message received.

My head shot up from where I stared at my phone to see Banner turning on the driveway.

Only something wasn't right because he always ran until reaching the porch.

He was walking, slowly, one hand clutching his head while the other hung at his side.

"Banner!"

It was that feeling again, my chest tightening as he seemed to walk even slower after I called out his name, his head lifting slowly to meet my gaze. The pain in even that simple motion was plain to see.

No.

"No, no, no."

The words rushed out of my mouth, a verbal denial of the moment playing out before my eyes, as he stopped walking. Slowly raising his other hand to his head, as if he was nearly too weak to even do that, came right before his knees gave out and he collapsed onto the pavement.

With a scream, I rushed to his side and called 9-1-1, tears streaming down my face as I silently begged him not to die.

BREATHING BECAME SOMETHING I HAD TO REMIND myself to do.

I played today back in my head, over and over, not quite understanding how things could have started off so hopeful yet ended in such an awful way.

Clutching Banner's things, I had to force myself to listen as the doctor explained how there hadn't been anything they could've done to save his life. How Banner had died from a ruptured brain aneurysm.

Even though I heard the words, I wasn't able to comprehend how that could possibly happen in an otherwise healthy man in his early thirties. That question wasn't one anybody would probably ever be able to answer for me.

I didn't know what to do after he left the room. The doctor told me to take as long as I needed, but my gaze wouldn't move from my lap. I couldn't bear to see him that way, even if I had managed to accept he wouldn't be going home with me.

Maybe I should have touched him, held his hand, given him one last kiss, but bringing myself to do that proved impossible.

That wasn't Banner. He wasn't here anymore.

Eventually, I stood up and kept my gaze averted, signing the papers the doctors left next to me before rushing out of the room, my chest heavy with all the suppressed emotions. My determination to make it back home, into privacy, before letting my grief run free kept me upright as I headed out of the hospital's front doors.

Tugging my phone out of my pocket, I ordered a ride, my fingers shaking the whole time, and that's when I realized that I hadn't called Banner's mother yet.

Judy would be devastated. I knew that and it was one of the reasons I didn't call right then. Considering it was nearly midnight now, she would be in bed or about to go to bed. There wasn't anything she could do; it was even too late to get a flight out of the airport.

In my head, it was kinder and more thoughtful to give her one more night where she believed her son was alive, safe and sound at home with his wife. Not lying lifeless in a hospital bed.

Her night wouldn't be anything like mine.

I was going home to an empty house, one where even in the moments before Banner collapsed in the driveway, I had been positive and thinking about the future.

And when I finally arrived there, the slight smell of our

untouched dinner remained in the air. I didn't remember coming back in to turn off the stove, even after the ambulance arrived, so somebody else must have done that.

But that smell was the reminder of what would never be again.

That's all it took for all my banked emotions to burst forward and I sunk to the floor, gasping for air as the tears came hard and fast. I didn't feel anything around me, not even the hardness of the wood against my knees, because the reality of what happened finally washed over me.

I cried until no more tears would come, until the physical pain from lying on the floor while curled into a ball became unbearable. Even as I slowly rose to my feet, my whole body shook and the wall supported me until there wasn't any doubt my legs would get me to my room, if no further.

After climbing the stairs, I made it to the bedroom and froze in the doorway. My feet tried to move while my brain was unwilling to allow me any further inside the room. His scent would be on the sheets and pillows. I thought I would want that comfort, but no matter how hard I tried, I couldn't make myself actually get anywhere near it.

Turning around, I headed toward the guest room and climbed into bed, believing there wasn't any way I would sleep tonight.

But within minutes, the worse day of my life ended as I drifted off into a fitful slumber.

CHAPTER 28

FEBRUARY 9TH

Banner's phone was ringing.

I didn't understand why he didn't answer it. I rolled over, seeking his warm body in order to poke him in the side so he would answer the damn call, but he wasn't there.

The ringing stopped.

For a moment, I wondered where he was, until the reality of what happened last night slammed its way back into my brain. Bolting upright as the phone rang again, I hopped out of the bed and rushed over to the bag that held his things. My breath caught at the sight of "Mom" on his phone screen.

Throat tightening, there wasn't anything to do except answer his phone, because I knew she would keep calling until he answered. Tapping the accept button, I lifted the phone to my ear and forced words past my trembling lips. "Hi, Aunt Judy."

"Valerie?"

Her confused yet cheerful question made me wince. I nodded for a second, then cleared my throat because of course she couldn't see me and whispered, "Yes. I... um..."

"Sorry, darling. You don't typically answer his phone." She paused and when I didn't reply, asked, "Is he in the shower? Is that why you're answering for him?"

My throat tightened more, almost unbearably. Tears sprung to my eyes and I had to grit my teeth to shove my way past the emotion to say, "No. I'm... I'm sorry, Judy. Last night, he... something happened."

He was dead. I should have said the words, but I didn't. That didn't seem to matter because she was his mother and she grasped what I meant even though I couldn't voice them.

Her devastated cry... if my heart weren't already shattered, her sobs of despair would've had the same impact.

Because I didn't know how to comfort her when I couldn't even help myself, I merely repeated, "I'm sorry."

Her sobs grew into howls as she said, "I don't understand."

"Me neither."

It was honest. I had no idea how it happened and never would. If she wanted answers, she was bound to be as disappointed as I had been when the doctor gave me the news.

After a few minutes, she sniffled, her voice rising and firming as she said, "I will be there by the evening to take care of things. You'll let me do that for my son, won't you?"

As his wife, I knew taking care of everything was my place, but she was his mother. We both loved Banner and I knew he wouldn't want me to fight with her about anything.

And the last thing I wanted was that, because there wasn't any fight left in me now. The love of my life was gone; who made the arrangements was the least of my concerns.

"Yes, of course."

Not even bothering to say anything else, she hung up once I'd uttered the words. Not even a half hour later, my phone was blowing up with calls from everyone Banner knew, with one notable exception: my mother.

Not desiring to speak with anyone, I ignored all the calls and did the only thing I could think of in order to be alone...

I shut off my phone and his, then returned to the bed, where I planned to stay until his mother arrived.

WHEN JUDY WALKED INTO MY BEDROOM, SHE FOUND me sitting on the bed. I was sobbing into my hands after remembering today would have been our three-year wedding anniversary.

"Oh, darling."

I expected a lot of things upon her arrival, such as anger at my not calling her when I first got to the hospital last night, or any other negative emotion she thought to aim my way because she thought I deserved it.

But, no. Her sadness was clear and her affection washed over me, as did her comfort when she sat on the bed and wrapped me in her arms. Together, we wept, and I clung to her, seeking anything to anchor me as she stroked my hair.

Eventually, I was able to compose myself enough to pull away and grab some tissues from off the nightstand. We both wiped our eyes as she leaned back against the pillows, closing her eyes with a sigh.

After a few moments, she cleared her throat and softly inquired, "What happened?"

I didn't believe I would be able to tell her everything without breaking down again, but managed to say, "He collapsed in the driveway after his run. He was holding his head..."

Her lips flattened as she shook her head. "Those damn headaches. He told me they weren't anything to worry about."

"That's what the doctor said. He couldn't have

known." I used every ounce of willpower I had to push the tears back and keep my own lips from quivering as I continued, "It was an aneurysm. They tried to save him in the ambulance but... there wasn't much that could be done to help him by that point."

A beat of silence, then, "Where is he now?"

"The funeral home. We can go there in the morning."

She nodded, then sniffled, her eyes filling with tears again. "You waited to tell me on purpose."

"I couldn't imagine waking you up to tell you..."

"I understand, darling. I did the same when Paul had his heart attack. There was nothing Banner could have done until the next day and the hours waiting to come see his father would have been unbearable."

We fell into a brief silence before she sighed and whispered, "Thank you."

"For what?"

"For not listening to your mother and I. For loving my son and making him happy."

Not what I expected her to say, let alone thank me for. Turning my head, I found her staring at me, silent tears sliding down her cheeks. Reaching for her hand, I clasped it in mine and told her, "My heart wouldn't let me love anyone else. He made me happy, too. I don't know how I'll live without him."

"You just will, darling." She clucked her tongue and

swiped a tear from her face with her free hand. "The pain gets easier to manage with time."

That's what I heard. That's what people told me after my father died, too. It never got any easier when I tried to call him only to realize he wouldn't be the one answering the phone ever again.

And I had Banner to help me through the hard time that had come after, for the months when random moments sent me to bed, where I curled into a ball while crying for my father.

This time, he wouldn't be here, the man who was also the source of my grief. I didn't know how to tell his mother that this wasn't anything like I had ever experienced before. My chest was hollow and I was drowning from the inside out.

Everything I ever read said someone else shouldn't be your everything, that you had to be able to stand on your own, but I hated that bullshit. I could hold a job, I could have a life outside of him; I had for many years before we met.

Who would anybody be to tell me that he wasn't my entire world, couldn't be my everything, when that's exactly what he had been? He was the love of my life. The one I kept going back to over and over no matter how much I fought the inevitable. There wasn't any way this grief would ever lessen or lighten.

He always wanted me with him, desired nothing more than for me to choose him and be together. And now, I wanted to be with him, even if that meant not breathing any longer, because the days before me... fuck, they were long and endless.

One day, then another, where I would wake up thinking he should be beside me, only to relive through the grief every morning when I realized he wouldn't be there. Never, ever again would we kiss, talk, hug, or make love. I would never feel his bare skin against mine, my head on his chest listening to his heart beat wildly after sex. He would never wrap his arms around me to hold me close and tell me how much he loved me. I would never again hear him say how much he couldn't wait until we were alone again so he could show me. Nor would he be able to tell me everything would be all right when I felt like everything was falling apart.

No.

That was all gone. He wasn't ever coming back, and even though I know he hadn't meant to, he had left me alone after promising me I would never be without him again.

I wished I could tell her that she was right, that time would make the hurt easier, but I couldn't.

And although I gave her a small smile when she squeezed my hand in reassurance since I hadn't responded to what she said, on the inside there wasn't any reason to smile.

I knew it wouldn't be long before I finally gave into the despair; before living without him became unbearable to the point I couldn't handle it anymore.

INSTEAD OF CELEBRATING ANOTHER YEAR TOGETHER, Banner's mother arranged his funeral.

I managed to force myself out of bed to attend, but only barely.

Standing next to his mother, I stared at his casket, and at the hole his body would soon be lowered into. Tears streamed down my cheeks at recalling how I laughed at him when he told me about purchasing us plots so when we died, we would be buried next to each other.

At the time, I wondered why he would worry about something like that when we were so young. He told me he wanted to make sure we would never be separated again, even in death.

How wrong he had been.

He died and I remained living. He wasn't breathing anymore and my heart continued to beat even though I wished it wouldn't. Every time my eyes closed these past few days, I hoped they would never open again.

And each morning, disappointment led to sobbing my eyes out at waking up alone. To rediscovering he wasn't lying beside me and never would be again.

We had become separated.

He was gone. He left me alone after promising me I would never be without him again.

And I couldn't even summon the energy to get angry because he hadn't meant to leave me behind. He saw a doctor, he tried to make sure he remained healthy for our life together, and in the end, none of that mattered.

Even after the funeral ended, I drifted through the day. Although I wanted nothing more than to go home and stay in bed forever, Judy made sure to keep me by her side for the gathering at our house afterward.

The house filled up with some people I knew, but mostly ones I didn't. After a while, I tried to excuse myself from the constant barrage of people telling me how sorry they were.

I didn't get far before my mother took over making sure I wasn't alone, pulling up a chair to sit beside me. She took my hand in hers, holding tight even when I attempted to tug free, and remained there in silence despite all the things I was certain she wished to say to me.

Why she did this, I had no clue. We hadn't spoken in years, especially after my marriage to Banner. The fact she even showed up for the funeral surprised me, until I acknowledged she did it for Judy, not for me.

I disappointed her over my refusal to give up my relationship with Banner, then broke her heart when we moved away and married each other. I tried, though, to keep her included, because when I told Banner I didn't want her funeral to be the next time we were in each other's lives, I meant that.

The fact she was here now would have meant more to me if she had been there for me and Banner when he was alive. If she hadn't cut me out of her life until I was willing to cut him out of mine, then perhaps I would be willing to take comfort in her presence.

Not now.

What I wanted more than anything was to go curl into my bed and be alone. I needed all these people to leave this house, leave me in peace. But I said nothing, because it wouldn't last long and soon they would be gone.

And when they finally did go, leaving me faced with concern from my mother as well as Judy?

My mother went into the kitchen to prepare us all something to eat, while Judy sat beside me and held my hands in hers. "Perhaps the best course of action at this point is for you to return home, darling."

"No." There wasn't any way I would ever go home again. "I'm not going back to Ohio with either of you. This is my home and has been for years."

"Val—"

"No!" With that, I shook off her hold and stood up, tears streaming down my cheeks again as I glared at her. My mother had returned to the room by the time I was able to speak again. "Both of you just go away. This was my home with Banner. I'm not leaving, you can't fucking make me, and I'm not going to talk about this any longer."

My mother opened her mouth, then closed it, and for some reason, this pissed me off even more.

"What?" I hissed at her, arms crossed over my chest. "Did you really think now that he died I would be happy to come back home? Is that why you're here?"

Her whole face blanched as she shook her head. "That's an awful thing to say, Val. And—"

"Oh! I'm the awful one? You're the one who refused to see me or speak to me because of my relationship with Banner." I point at her and then toward the foyer. "You need to get the fuck out of my house."

"I'm worried about you." Her lips trembled as she took a step forward and nodded at Judy. "We're both concerned. Judy says you've not eaten much since she arrived."

Of course they talked about me. These two were thick as thieves and had been since Banner and I's relationship began. "I'm an adult. What I do and don't do isn't either of your concern. And I want you to leave. Now."

As they stood there, staring at each other as if they

could telepathically decide what to do next, that's when I lost what little control I had left.

"Get out!" I screamed at them while turning to grab a vase off a shelf nearby and hurting it across the room, where it hit the wall and shattered. My whole body trembled from the rage coursing throughout. All ability to cope with this on top of everything else was gone as I pointed toward the front door once more. "Both of you just need to leave me the fuck alone."

They did.

Both left without another word and within minutes, I crawled into the bed I shared with Banner, ready to sleep.

No crying.

No feelings at all.

Just numbness as I curled up into a ball and went to sleep because there wasn't anything else for me to do now.

* * *

"Do we need to take her to the hospital?"

God, that was Sam's voice.

I didn't want to see anyone.

Why were they here? Didn't they understand I didn't want anyone around, including them?

Friends or not, why wouldn't everyone simply leave me be? None of them could understand what I was going through.

"No. She's still breathing." Sarah tapped my cheek once, sighing. "Val, get up."

I didn't want to answer. I knew if I didn't, though, that they might call 9-1-1 and I definitely didn't want that sort of attention.

So, despite wanting to scream for them to leave me alone and get out, I opened my eyes slowly.

And fuck, did the motion burn. The sun hurt. Everything did now.

Existing was the worst.

"There you go." Sarah smiled at me and sat next to me on the bed. Well, as much as she could in the small edge available. "We came over yesterday but you didn't answer."

I remembered them knocking, but most of my day had been spent in bed. I hadn't eaten anything, only drank a few cups of water.

Not that it seemed to help. My mouth was dry, so not even licking my lips helped as I croaked, "How did you get in?"

Sam held up a key. "Banner gave me this for emergencies."

Of course he had. Banner thought of everything.

Well, that is, except for what would become of his wife when he wasn't around any longer.

"Come home with us," Sarah pleaded softly. "Please. You can stay as long as you like, Val. That way you aren't alone."

"Thanks, but I'm fine."

"You're not."

I didn't like the way Sarah's eyes filled with tears as she reached out to cover my hand with hers. Worse was the emptiness in my chest, the numbness that made her pain unable to penetrate the haze around me.

"Please, Val. I'm worried."

"Don't be." I withdrew my hand and grabbed the blanket, dragging it up to my face. "He's gone. Why won't everyone just fucking let me be sad?"

"You can be sad, Val, but you still have to eat. And shower."

"I will, okay? Just... not today. Okay?"

"All right.

I knew Sarah well and she didn't believe me. But what could she do? What could anyone do?

I peeked from beneath the covers as she finally stood up and leaned over to give me a loose hug. "We need to return home now, but call me if you need me. Please?"

Good. It was better for her to return to her son and the great life she had with Sam. Better than being here with me when I didn't want anyone around.

So I could promise her that much, even with no plans to call her or anyone else because they weren't the person I needed. "I will."

"Love ya."

Upon waking up later that evening, I couldn't remember whether or not I told Sara that I loved her, too.

But it was a fleeting thought because the torturous pain of missing Banner remained and all I wanted was to know if it dying would be the only way it would stop.

CHAPTER 30

MAYBE THINGS WOULD HAVE BEEN DIFFERENT IF I hadn't turned off both of our phones the morning after he died.

Nobody could talk to me unless they stopped by in person. Even then I ignored their knocks because I didn't want to see or speak with anyone.

Perhaps if somebody had been able to force me to get help? What if they had been able to prove I might be a danger to myself and make the nearby hospital admit me to their psych ward?

That's the thing about being an adult though. With a few exceptions, no one can force another loved one to get the help they might need, no matter how much they spiral out of control.

Maybe the key was that I wasn't hurting anyone else. I

wasn't out driving drunk or acting recklessly. Wasn't drawing attention to how bad things had become.

I laid at home in bed, eating and drinking at the bare minimum. We had enough alcohol to last me for months although I didn't drink much of it. Some nights I drank a little bit, staring at the bottle and wondering whether downing the whole thing would make me feel better.

Honestly, though, would getting help do any good? Not even in my most sober moments did I believe talking to someone would help me.

Nothing would lift me out of this deep sadness, or take away the years yawning in front of me where he wasn't with me. No amount of talking would bring him back to life or allow me to kiss him, talk to him, and hug him.

Never again would his skin be against mine, or would I be able to rest my head on his chest and listen to his heartbeat. He wouldn't wrap his arms around me, hold me close as he whispered how much he loved me and couldn't wait until we're alone, so he could show me.

I didn't want to live without the man who loved me even when I couldn't love myself.

Nor could I see past the pain or imagine going another day where he wasn't here with me.

Yes, I knew why my mother and Judy insisted I return home. And why Sarah told me I could come stay with her and Sam if I wanted.

Reminders of Banner surrounded me by staying in this house. Our home was just that — *our* home. And I saw him everywhere I went. No matter what room was entered, I would picture him standing there or walking toward me or smiling at me in invitation from where he sat.

The memories — and thus the pain — were constant.

But I didn't want to go anywhere else either.

How could leave the home he bought for us? The one he wanted us to spend the rest of our lives in?

None of them understood this was all I had left of Banner and my pain wasn't ever going to end as long as he wasn't here beside me.

That's how I ended up on the floor, after taking almost an entire bottle of sleeping pills. They were a leftover bottle from a bad patch of anxiety I had last year, although I hadn't ended up taking more than two or three of them.

I saw the bottle in the cupboard, looked into the mirror at myself, and didn't recognize the woman staring back at me. I was hollow. Numb. A shadow of the happy woman from almost two weeks ago who kissed her husband in the kitchen less than an hour before he died.

So I grabbed the pills and held them tight in my fist while walking to the kitchen. Found a bottle with the highest proof alcohol I could and walked into the living room.

God, I stared at them both for hours. Not because I

didn't comprehend the enormity of what I was about to do. The thoughts flying through my head were more about what would happen if this didn't work. If I didn't die, just made myself really sick to the point I would wish for death even more.

My decision had been made though. I wasn't going to back out because the alternative was worse in my mind.

And within hours I was laying on the floor with my phone in my hand, staring up at the ceiling as my life slowly drifted away.

I had grabbed it because I wanted to hear his voice one last time using the single voicemail saved on it.

My eyes burned as the screen flashed while starting up. It took everything I had to focus, to press the phone icon and then click on voicemail. Who knew my hands would shake this badly?

I always loved having visual voicemail. Seeing his name, I clicked on it and listened to the last message he sent me, earlier in that day when he was at work.

Pressing the play button, I clicked on speaker, and tears streamed down my cheeks at the sound of his voice after way too long. *"Hey, sweetheart. I know you're in a meeting. Just called to say I'll be home at the usual time. I love you."*

Then I played it again. And once more before the sight of more voicemails caught my attention. I knew there would be a lot of people who called, which is why I shut my phone off in the first place, but was that...?

I raised one hand to mouth, gasping at the sight of the name and number of my doctor's office. I had forgotten all about going there and why.

I pressed the button, waiting for her to tell me what the tests said, and what was really wrong with me.

That's when the sobs increased, when I cried so hard I had trouble breathing.

Fuck.

Fuck.

How had everything gotten so messed up?

Each second of what came next became a blur as the haziness and dizziness heightened, the ceiling spinning faster and faster above me.

I didn't recall calling 9-1-1, except for the slight buzzing of a woman's voice trying to get my attention on the phone.

The only thing I could do was fight to keep my eyes open despite the increasing desire to close them. They hurt so bad... until I couldn't ignore the impulse any longer.

That's when I saw Banner.

He waited for me, with his hand held out, and I reached for him hoping he would forgive me for what I had done.

Our fingertips brushed as the permanent darkness I

had craved settled behind my eyelids. My body was heavy from the pills and alcohol coursing through my system. And my entire soul was ready to leave this life behind for an eternity with the love of my life.

As his hand closed around mine, his eyes and lips smiled in welcome as I began to slip into unconsciousness.

That's when the faint sound of sirens grew louder while a buzzing sound grew inside my head. The light shined brighter, too, beckoning me to leave this world and all my pain behind.

I knew they were coming for me and they would probably be too late.

"I'm sorry."

The words rang loudly in my head and in the air even though I whispered them to the empty room.

As the buzzing in my head grew louder, I heard the sound of faint footsteps slapping against our wooden floors, headed in my direction.

And with what little energy remained, I whispered the one thing I hoped would still be true if they were able to save me.

"Help me. I'm pregnant and don't want to die."

THE END

Thanks for reading! I hope you'll continue on and check out the afterword.

Visit my website to join my reader's list and stay up-to-date on new releases, giveaways, events & more. No spam ever!

Afterword

First, let me make this clear: this book is fiction and none of the actions taken in this book by any character are condoned or suggested by me.

If you or a loved one are talking about or considering suicide, you should seek the proper help. In the USA, you can call the National Suicide Prevention Lifeline at 1-800-273-8255 or contact them by chatting online here. They are open 24/7. And if you live elsewhere, check out this list here.

With that said, you might be wondering… wait… what the hell? Did she live or die?

As for the answer to the question above… I don't know. Did she survive or not?

That's up to you, dear reader.

There is no epilogue and no sequel. I spent years writing this story, leaving, and coming back to write again. This is how the story ends. When I try to write past this, nothing happens, so therefore, I don't have an answer for you.

And I hope you'll be okay with filling in the blanks on your own. Sometimes... we just don't know what comes next.

I wish you well. Please feel free to contact me if you wish to (respectfully, please) at violet@authorvi-olethaze.com. I'm always open to receiving emails from my readers!

<3 Violet

ABOUT THE AUTHOR

Violet Haze is a big fan of reading and writing romance.
The autistic mother of one, she currently lives in Ohio and
is self-employed. When not working or writing, she spends
her days reading, procrastinating, & listening to her son
play video games she doesn't understand, at all.

For information on other books you can read, including
links to ALL the vendors, visit her website: www.
authorviolethaze.com!

Want to contact Violet?
Email her at: violet@authorviolethaze.com or locate her at
one of the links listed below!

Violet is also on Patreon and would love to see you there!